ROLLING IN CLOVER

Rolling In Clover

...She slid her hand into his firm grasp. "Kimberley."

"Let's take a walk. You want to?"

Of all the things she wanted to do with this man—was she crazy? She didn't even know him!—walking was among the most innocent, but she shook her head. "I should go home."

He pulled away his hand—she probably should have released it already—and twisted his wedding band. "I'm not trying to pick you up. I'm married. Harmless." He hitched his chin toward the rear exit of the club. "Come on."

As if he were the Pied Piper, she followed. Had she lost her mind?

"So, your third, huh?" He held open the door, and standing in the bright rays of sunshine, he looked like a savior carved into a cathedral wall.

"Third pregnancy, second child." She exited into the tranquil April day, catching a whiff of peppermint and fabric softener in his wake.

He clucked his tongue and climbed over a split-rail fence into a thicket of prairie plants. "Sorry, miscarriage is rough. My wife and I never had to deal with that, but my sister Julie's had two. I can't imagine what you went through."

"Actually..." She bit her tongue. A perfect stranger—and *perfect*, he was, from his defined, muscled torso threatening to shred his threadbare T-shirt, to his long, sinewy legs—was hardly an appropriate sounding board for her regrets regarding Jason Devon's child...

PRAISE FOR ROLLING IN CLOVER

"Right from the start *Rolling in Clover* packs a one-two whammy of expertly turned phrases and perfect imagery. This is not an ooey-gooey romance with fluttering eyes and rippling pecs. Penny Dawn has penned a story with depth and emotion that will leave any reader eagerly devouring page after page."

—Megan Hart,
Award-winning Author

"Penny Dawn draws you into a tale of two people struggling to find happiness in the choices they've made…You don't want to leave them until they've gotten it right. Fill up before you start reading, because you won't be able to eat past the lump in your throat."

—Natalie J. Damschroder
Author of *Kira's Best Friend*

ALSO BY PENNY DAWN

Making Noise
Measuring Up
Salute
Sound-Off

ROLLING IN CLOVER

BY

PENNY DAWN

AMBER QUILL PRESS, LLC
http://www.amberquill.com

ROLLING IN CLOVER
AN AMBER QUILL PRESS BOOK

This book is a work of fiction. All names, characters, locations, and incidents are products of the author's imagination, or have been used fictitiously. Any resemblance to actual persons living or dead, locales, or events is entirely coincidental.

Amber Quill Press, LLC
http://www.amberquill.com

All rights reserved.
No portion of this book may be transmitted or reproduced in any form, or by any means, without permission in writing from the publisher, with the exception of brief excerpts used for the purposes of review.

Copyright © 2006 by Penny Dawn Steffen
ISBN 1-59279-736-9
Cover Art © 2006 Trace Edward Zaber

Layout and Formatting provided by: ElementalAlchemy.com

PUBLISHED IN THE UNITED STATES OF AMERICA

Acknowledgements

When I began this novel, I had no idea how emotionally draining a task I'd undertaken. I couldn't have done it without:

My husband, who supports me in this wild and wacky endeavor. He's a vice much healthier than nicotine.

My girls, who are prizes at the end of the rainbow, and whose wardrobe rampages inspired Allison Colleen's.

My extended family, which taught me every good family hides skeletons in its closets.

My good friend and very talented writer, Jillicious, who offered sage advice to develop Brennan's character. She rounded out that man...and he didn't even have to give her a diamond. Thanks, Jill!

Jacki King, who provides immeasurable moral support always and is often my sounding board for new ideas and options. She's also an ace with a spreadsheet, chock full of hunky hunks.

My editor, EJ, who held my hand as Brennan's addictions grew, and grew, and grew.

Officer Brian Ernst of the Grayslake PD, without whom I'd be clueless when it came to DUI regulations and other domestic disputes. You're in for a little Rolling In Clover, *yourself, Officer. Congratulations on your engagement.*

Attorney D. Del Re, who shared his knowledge of Family Law.

Kimberley Howe, fellow MIRA Scholar, who shared her name with my heroine.

My cold readers—Mary, Li'l Kristin, and the goddess Angela—and the rest of my girlfriends, who each had a hand—however, unknowingly—in plotting this novel. It takes a world of women to concoct the abyss of woes in which my Kimberley swims...

Additional thanks to Trace for designing such yummy covers.

And to: Faculty of Seton Hill University, for pointing the way; Grayslake Curves, for providing a fabulous network for all women striving to achieve their goals; The members of Tuesday night ladies' dance class, for incredible support. Thanks, all, for believing in me.

*For my mother, Star,
who has never been afraid to remodel a kitchen—
and is equally unafraid of changing her
life...for the better.*

CHAPTER 1

"Can you feel my cock?"

The gruff words needled Kimberley Roderick's reverie like hail against a sun-bathed window. Through a fog of sleep, her husband emerged before her—glassy-eyed, disheveled, and climbing between her legs.

The acrid combination of whiskey and sweat oozed from his pores. She turned her cheek to his mouth and fought her gag reflex with a slow exhalation. "Wait, Brennan."

"Can you feel it, baby?" His clammy hands pinned her wrists into the pillows, imprisoning her against their king-sized mattress, and he nudged his way between her thighs, forcing her legs to part. "Tell me you want it. Tell me you love it."

The sloppy, pickled kiss at the corner of her lips fueled her will to escape. "Get off me." His grip burned a ring around her wrists when she twisted away.

The scent of the ninth green sifted through the room on a cool spring breeze, as if promising tranquility. But when it swept over her flesh, moist with her husband's sweat, an uncomfortable chill settled on her.

Amid the dim stream of porch light filtering through the sheers, his midnight blue eyes revealed no trace of the man she'd met at the altar eight years ago. "Can you feel my cock?"

"Stop already." Raw pain zinged her left wrist where the heel of his palm entrapped her. "You're hurting me."

"Can you feel it? Do you want it?"

"What can you do with it, in this condition?" With gritted teeth and force enough to tip his balance, she tore her left arm free from his weight and scrambled out from under him.

"Whoa." A hearty laugh accompanied his tumble to the yellow-and-white striped Waverly sheets, his half-flaccid penis drooping out the fly of his boxer shorts and his head coming to rest on a fluffy pillow. "Feisty tonight."

"I'm pregnant, for God's sake." She was only a few weeks along, but pregnant was pregnant. With a swift yank, she zipped the pillow out from under his head. "And you have a problem."

"Grow up."

Interesting advice from a thirty-two-year-old man acting like a frat boy. There were only two circumstances in which he'd return home in such a state. He didn't drink in excess unless he'd gambled and lost big, or gambled and won huge. Neither cause was any more attractive than the end result.

She spied and retrieved a withdrawal receipt amid the pile of clothing her husband had abandoned on the floor. Three thousand dollars. And not more than sixty left in his pockets. An expensive buzz.

"Love you, Kimmy Coco Bop."

"I hate that nickname."

"Kimmy, Kimmy Coco Bop," he crooned, performing a horizontal version of the 1950s pony dance. "Kimmy, Kimmy Bop."

Up against another woman, she'd fight tooth and nail for Brennan, but his addictive personality was one mistress with whom she could never compete. And she had scars on her heart to prove it.

She fingered the crocheted lace on the pillow case—so intricate—and turned away.

"Where you going?" His voice sounded gravelly and his words slurred. "Missed you this week, baby."

"Apparently not enough." His plane had touched down at O'Hare International Airport fourteen hours earlier, thirty minutes before the season opener at Wrigley Field. He'd probably charmed the hell out of his friends in that sky box, but at 3:24 in the morning, stinking drunk, no magic remained for Kimberley.

Can you feel my cock? She'd cut the son-of-a-bitch off just as soon as she'd touch it tonight.

"Kimmmmmmy."

With the expanse of soft, white carpeting in their bedroom behind her, she pressed a hand to her still-flat abdomen and sauntered down the walnut herringbone path, goose-down pillow in tow. She paused outside their three-year-old daughter's bedroom.

Allison Colleen's raven curls, soft and bouncy, spilled over a rosebud pillowcase, and she rubbed the worn satin ears of a stuffed, pink rabbit against her summer-peach cheek. *Innocent. Gorgeous.*

Not twelve hours ago, the child had fingered the prominent diamond in Kimberley's wedding band, spinning it around her mother's finger as if she knew of its impermanence.

"Love you, Allie," Kimberley now whispered, blowing a kiss toward the princess canopy bed.

Children. They were nothing short of treasures, gifts. And Kimberley had already given one back to God. Such an egotistical, foolish decision, but a sacrifice she'd chosen to make for the sake of a life of her own.

And some life it was.

She'd graduated *summa cum laude* and had a brief but stunning career in family law. And now, she served Cheerios. She was a smart woman trapped in a miniscule corner of a massive, flourishing world, about to bring another child into it.

When two bright blue lines appeared on the pregnancy test last week, she should have pulled her application from the University of Illinois at Chicago. With two small children and a husband with addictions, she'd never have time to teach at UIC. The commute alone would consume every moment of her free time. Not that they'd call her for an interview anyway. She'd been out of the loop too long.

She dragged her pillow down the rear staircase, seeking a tiny slice of Eden among her frustrations. Serenity resided on the highest shelf above twin Subzero refrigerators, which had been paneled to resemble an oversized, cherry armoire, complete with carved moldings and antique pulls. In her favorite cookbook, opposite a creamy hollandaise recipe, she kept memories of a less complicated era and the truest connection a man and a woman could possibly share.

In the first-floor guest suite, the plush, sage duvet on the Timberlake bed comforted her tired body. She opened *The Fabulous Gourmet*, grazing her fingers across worn stationery that read, "From the Desk of Jason Devon." The understated joke still evoked a smile. Unless bleachers in a high school gymnasium counted, Jason had never had a desk. A down-to-earth, wholesome American athlete, through and through. And Kimberley had had no right to abort his child.

She perused the letter Jason had delivered on the eve of her wedding, via courier. For the thousandth time, she read his words, or rather recited them while she stared at his handwriting. Sharp-ending strokes, nothing flowery about his script...or his subject matter.

Marrying a man who doesn't know thing one about you won't fill this void. Reconnect with your sisters, make peace with the only family you have. But don't take one step down that aisle. It'll be the biggest mistake of your life.

She closed her eyes and imagined her ex-lover's naked body between her thighs. In her mind, she and Jason were still in that summer of love.

Eleven years ago. Lehmann Beach, way past sundown. Sweat and Cedar Lake rained down on her, sprinkling from his golden hair. His stomach melted against hers in the intense summer heat, and her breasts tingled with the slightest brush against him. Her hands registered the flex of his lean buttocks when he thrust deep and slow and thorough, filling her completely, reaching depths unknown to any other man. She tensed beneath him, climbing to a glorious height. He sealed his mouth over hers, swallowing her pleasured cries in their public arena.

Soft, determined tongue teasing hers. Skilled lips roving her neck, her shoulders, and capable hands exploring the drenched mop atop her head, tickling down her sand-covered spine.

The days of Cedar Lake were long gone, sacrificed along with Jason's child. She was drowning in another life, while her husband swam at the bottom of a bottle, feeding one addiction after another.

"I don't stay because I'm weak," she whispered, trailing a finger along Jason's letter. "I stay because I'm strong. It's important you understand that."

* * *

In the dim light of dawn, Lucas Jackson opened a door in his modest hallway and peered into a bedroom decorated with purple butterflies. Rachael's five-year-old fingers mindlessly twirled a shredded piece of white satin, the only remnant of a cherished baby blanket, in her sleep. He'd grown to love her. It wasn't her fault she wasn't his.

He'd named her and cut her umbilical cord, for God's sake, and that's all that mattered. Well, that and forgiveness, his constant challenge. With the help of a snot-nosed therapist, whom Luke doubted knew much about women, and much less about marriage, he would work through the anger, let go of the hurt.

As quietly as possible, he closed his would-be daughter's door and walked along a worn path in the carpeting to the next room, where Caleb, his eldest, still slept. Luke sat on the edge of the bed and placed a hand on his son's back. The dinosaur pajamas were far too small, but they were Caleb's favorites.

Children became attached to things quickly and unpredictably. Luke had become attached to their mother in much the same way, when he fell head first in love at the age of sixteen. A long time ago, she'd loved him, and God overcame the birth control pill, giving them the greatest gift in the world—his son.

Just outside Caleb's door, an ancient retriever awaited him, a golden tail wagging its own version of joy. Luke had adopted Derby in high school, and over the years, the dog had been a faithful companion. More faithful than his wife. And although every step likely challenged the dog, he accompanied his master down the stairs to the foyer.

Luke yanked a sweatshirt off the halltree he'd built last spring. He'd assembled the piece with painstaking care, routing the edges with an ogee bit, carefully rubbing the maple grain with a henna stain. At an antique hardware store in downtown Chicago, he'd found four wrought iron coat hooks and a vintage cup-pull for the mitten drawer under the seat.

When he'd completed the labor of love, Diane didn't thank him. "After years of dirt across my floor," she'd said, "it's about time you gave the kids a place to take off their shoes."

She now scuttled in the kitchen, slamming cabinet doors, slapping a towel against the countertop. "Do you think just once you can find the fucking dishwasher?"

Satan incarnate. The Discovery Channel had recently reported on the phenomenon early psychologists coined "hysteria." Premenstrual Syndrome transformed an ordinarily level-headed woman into a crazy person. Diane's PMS was constant, unrelenting.

"Look at this, will you?" She whipped a sponge into the sink, piled with his dinner dishes. "It isn't enough for me to clean up after the kids? I have to wipe your nose, too?"

He neglected to respond, simply slipped his arms into his jacket.

"If you can put some time aside," she said, "I'll explain the concept to you once again: dishes on the racks, soap in this convenient little compartment, turn the knob to on."

He'd like to turn a knob all right. Maybe he'd help out around the house if she'd sweeten the deal in the bedroom.

"Are you listening to me?" Six months older than he, she'd recently turned thirty-two. But the scowl in her eyes was that of an old, crotchety woman.

Over the years, her once-blonde hair had become dry and brassy, her complexion, sallow. She lost far too much weight after Rachael was born, making her bony and breastless. However, it was not her physical attributes—or lack thereof—that he'd found unattractive. When she rested in peaceful sleep, she was as beautiful as the day they'd met. In her continuous state of tirade, however, she might as well be adorned with green horns and a spiked tail.

"I said, are you listening to me?"

"Yes, Diane, I'm listening to you."

"Are you taking the dog out?"

"I'm going to work out," Luke said. "And then I have my session with Dr. Schaeffer."

"He's your damn dog."

Yeah, well, half of Rachael is some idiot's sperm, but I love her anyway. He turned toward the staircase, where Derby rested, filling the entire landing. He whistled a low tone. "Come on, boy."

The old pup lifted his head and meandered toward him. Diane had once loved Derby, too, had walked him up to Luke's football games, proudly displaying number eleven on her back. For six years after graduation, only the field and the game changed. Furlan's Field at the Fort Sheridan Reserve Base, where he played working man's softball. A peaceful, if not predictable life…until Uncle Sam had beckoned Luke to exotic Saudi Arabia.

And shortly after he'd returned, he and Diane learned that ninety-nine percent effective meant exactly what it sounded like. No time for games of any sort with his boy on the way.

"All right," Luke said, massaging Derby's ears when the dog perched at his feet. "You can wait in the truck. I'll leave it running with the heat on."

"That's all we need." Diane slammed the dishwasher shut. "Another through-the-roof bill on the gas card. It's not that cold out there, you know."

With a deep, tired sigh, Luke shoved his hands through his hair. He had to get out. Out of the house, out of this marriage, out of this life. But unlike a previous, monumental exit, in which he'd carried everything he owned out the door, this absence would encompass only an hour or two. He'd have to make the most of it. He couldn't live without his children.

Once Derby settled into the cab, taking up much of the bench seat, Luke twisted his wedding ring, and, for a fleeting second, he considered hiding it among the coins in the ashtray. He'd put it back on after his workout, in time for Dr. Know-It-All to pick his brain and place every blame in the world on his shoulders.

Halfway over his knuckle, he shoved the ring back on. Damn it, she was his wife. And as much as he wished he didn't, he loved her.

* * *

The gorgeous ornament on Kimberley's left hand, a symbol of the institution she'd once believed in, sparkled beneath the fluorescent lights in Gallant's Gym. Her stomach grumbled a reminder of its own—she hadn't eaten in a while—and the more she scrutinized her diamond, the more it became a blurred prism, racing around her head.

A yoga girl, she had no business waiting in line for a stair-stepper. Unfortunately, by the time Brennan had opened his hung-over eyes to watch Allison this morning, it was time for his weekly basketball league downtown, and, come whiskey or water, he never missed a chance to wager bucks for baskets. If she expected to make her class today, she should have anticipated the hangover and made other arrangements for their daughter earlier.

By the time she'd dropped Allison at her in-laws'—Brennan had promised to pick her up as soon as his game was over—the last yoga class was full, and she had no choice but to await a cardio-nightmare.

If not for the dreaded weight gain ahead of her, she might have forgone her exercise regimen for a bagel and decaffeinated raspberry tea at The Jasmine Vine, with UIC's fall class schedule open across the café table and her imagination running wild. Maybe if she taught at UIC, she'd bring more value to her family and more leverage to her marriage. And if she'd eaten this morning, she wouldn't be feeling so—

"Are you all right?" A crisp, baritone voice sounded over her right shoulder.

When she turned to acknowledge him, a wave of dizziness washed over her. She looked back to her hands. "Yes." She fixated on her ring, depending on the promises it held. If she looked away, even for a moment, she'd lose her balance amid the spinning, and if that man were half as tasty as he sounded, she might lose her senses.

Her heartbeat, a raging pulse at her temples, rattled her brain, and sweat broke on the back of her neck, accompanying a wave of nausea.

"You should sit down."

The world faded to black, and every body part numbed, save the crux of her arm, where a remarkable hand held her, a callused thumb tracing a circle on the inside of her elbow, four sand-paper fingers kneading into her flesh, coaxing blood flow. God, to feel hands like that in places she shouldn't...

The gym gradually came back into focus, and she blinked into the stranger's gaze. *Oh, my.* He stood about six-foot-two. Chocolate brown eyes, sandy brown hair, ultra white teeth. *Why the hell is he paying attention to me?* "I'm fine."

He shrugged a broad shoulder. "You don't seem to be." His mouth parted into a smile, and an electric surge shimmied through her veins, settling between her thighs, dancing on her clit. She knew it was purely physical attraction, but what a feeling. What would happen if those ambitious hands roved over the private terrain his smile had just unknowingly invaded?

"Want some water?"

Before she had a chance to reply, he lifted a bottle of Evian to her lips, pressing a hand to the back of her neck as she sipped. The heat of a wedding ring branded against her skin. *Married. Safe.*

She swallowed and forced herself to face him. "Thanks, I'm fine—"

"You nearly fell over."

"—just pregnant."

"Really?"

A crescent-shaped scar at the corner of his left eye crinkled with his illuminating smile. *Very distinguished.*

"Your first?"

"Third." Now why did she say that?

"Congratulations." He offered a tan hand, a red scrape at the base of his middle knuckle. "I'm Luke."

She slid her hand into his firm grasp. "Kimberley."

"Let's take a walk. You want to?"

Of all the things she wanted to do with this man—was she crazy? She didn't even know him!—walking was among the most innocent, but she shook her head. "I should go home."

He pulled away his hand—she probably should have released it already—and twisted his wedding band. "I'm not trying to pick you up. I'm married. Harmless." He hitched his chin toward the rear exit of the club. "Come on."

As if he were the Pied Piper, she followed. Had she lost her mind?

"So, your third, huh?" He held open the door, and standing in the bright rays of sunshine, he looked like a savior carved into a cathedral wall.

"Third pregnancy, second child." She exited into the tranquil April day, catching a whiff of peppermint and fabric softener in his wake.

He clucked his tongue and climbed over a split-rail fence into a thicket of prairie plants. "Sorry, miscarriage is rough. My wife and I never had to deal with that, but my sister Julie's had two. I can't imagine what you went through."

"Actually..." She bit her tongue. A perfect stranger—and *perfect*, he was, from his defined, muscled torso threatening to shred his threadbare T-shirt, to his long, sinewy legs—was hardly an appropriate sounding board for her regrets regarding Jason Devon's child.

"Where will you deliver?"

"Here. At Evanston Northwest." She perched her backside onto the fence and swung her legs over it, taking his proffered hand for balance and holding onto him a few moments longer than necessary when she dropped down on the other side. Hot, strong hands. Heaven against her back, she'd bet.

"Good hospital." He led her into a weaving of trees to a path. "When are you due?"

Geez, he walked fast. "Around Christmas."

"You're newly pregnant then."

"Just peed on the stick last week." *Great.* She'd known the man for three minutes, and already he knew she peed.

"Are you going to breastfeed?"

"Excuse me?"

"Breastfeeding. My wife did it. Are you going to?"

Although her breasts' activities were none of this man's business, her nipples hardened with his mentioning them. There was nothing sexual about breastfeeding an infant, but when she imagined Luke laving her with scrupulous patience, satisfaction pulsed through her. The image halted her in her tracks.

His mouth probably worked like mercury: burning, rising and

falling.

A beam of sunlight shot directly through hundreds of leaves and into her line of sight. "What did you say your wife's name was?"

"I didn't, but..." In a liquid movement, he turned to face her. "...it's Diane."

She shaded her eyes with a hand, stared up at him, and smiled in return. "Did Diane want to breastfeed, or did you pressure her into doing it? I mean, not that it's any of my business, Luke, but I think it's important for a woman to choose."

"I love an expressive woman." He cracked a smile. "We made the decision together."

Trees seemed to bend and whirl. She focused on the ground, but that spun, too.

"Easy." He grasped her under the elbow, leading her deeper into the shade of the deciduous trees. "Have a seat." He indicated the trunk of a fallen oak. Apparently, he knew this place well. Perhaps she was one of many women he'd led here. My God, she'd followed a serial adulterer.

"I run here," he said, as if he sensed her speculation. "Usually on Sundays."

Nauseated, she nodded, hoping she wouldn't vomit. God, how embarrassing would it be to toss her cookies right at his feet?

"Have some water." He brought his bottle to her lips, feeding her, massaging her arm where he held her. "Better?"

She wiped a dribble of water from her chin. "Fine."

He dropped to the forest floor before her and stretched, back to the ground, as if lying upon a raft on calm waters. The memory of Jason floating alongside her on Cedar Lake entered her mind. She attempted to blink the picture away, but, for the moment, Luke and Jason were one and the same. Comforting. Familiar.

"Too early for morning sickness, isn't it?" Luke asked.

"What?" She flinched from her meditation. "Yes. Mine usually begins at seven weeks and ends with the birth of a baby." *Or the termination of such.* "I'm just tired."

"Take a nap."

"And I haven't eaten in a while."

"Since when?"

The circumstances surrounding her recent fasting spun to the forefront of her mind: Brennan didn't come home with the dinner he'd promised last night. He was too ill to entertain Allison this morning, thus leaving little time for Kimberley to grab even a piece of fruit. His love affair with the fast lane had beaten out her pregnant appetite. Quite a feat. "Lunch yesterday."

"You know..." He yawned and sat up, looking her straight in the eyes. "I've never understood this crazy obsession with weight gain every pregnant woman seems to have."

"Evidently, no doctor has ever said 'watch your eating,' while probing two fingers to gauge the softness of *your* cervix."

"Touché." Again, his smile gleamed. "The only thing any doctor's going to probe of mine is my brain. And I'm not too crazy about that prospect either." He cleared his throat and his brow furrowed.

If he were on the witness stand, she would have recognized the expression as an invitation to spill information. She'd taken advantage of provocations such as this in the past. An occupational hazard, a cross all lawyers bear. But she resisted the urge to ask the next, most obvious question: *Why are you seeing a shrink?*

"Shame on your doctor," Luke said. "Hell, I'd gain two hundred pounds if it meant having a healthy baby."

"So would I."

"Then eat. As much as you want, whenever you want. Think about why you aren't eating, and wave goodbye to the bias. That tiny reason in your womb's more important."

What a tender thing to say. Why couldn't her husband say things like that? Tears welled in her eyes, but hiding them would be of no use. Too weak to fight them and too defeated to care, she wiped a drop from her cheek. "I haven't eaten because my husband is cheating on me." Did she just say that? To a stranger?

"Are you sure?" Luke dared to catch a tear on his finger. "Statistics show that one out of three husbands sleeps around during pregnancy, but I think expectant mothers assume their husbands cheat because sex becomes nonexistent."

Tears blurred her vision, but she locked her gaze on his intriguing mouth. "That's not it."

"It's true. I saw it on the Discovery Channel. You're figuring he has to get it somewhere, and since he's afraid to get it from you in this condition—"

"That's not the problem."

"Pregnancy gives women a pure and true glow. It isn't that your husband doesn't want you, believe me. But he sees you differently now, like the Virgin Mary maybe."

"That's an awfully personal inference. Who says I believe in the

Virgin Mary anyway?"

"I'm just saying he's probably not cheating on you." He leaned back on his elbows and yanked a leaf off a wild, green vine. "I know a beautiful woman when I see one." He shrugged and sipped his water. "He isn't cheating on you."

Had this headache pained her all morning? She pressed her fingers to her temples. Did he just tell her he thought she was...beautiful? She'd been cute, she'd been good-looking, but she'd never been pretty, and she'd certainly never been beautiful before. "I beg your pardon?"

"You're a beautiful woman," he said. "Your husband isn't cheating on you."

"My husband may not be getting blowjobs from his secretary, but he's still cheating on me."

"Did you say blowjobs? Can you say it again?"

"I should go."

"No, really. I kind of like the way you say it. I always wish my wife would set an alarm for herself and wake me with the ultimate blowjob."

"That's hardly any business of mine."

"I wouldn't mind waking up in the morning with a soft tongue treating me right. Have you ever wakened your husband that way?"

"And that's hardly any business of yours. Thanks for the walk, but I have to—"

His grip on her wrist sustained her. "I'm sorry if I offended you."

Her skin tingled beneath his touch, and the concern in his gaze stirred butterflies in her stomach. "I'm sorry I mentioned it." She ought to learn not to start things she couldn't finish—like applying to UIC, like raising the subject of oral sex with a beautiful stranger.

"I have places to go, too. And a dog in the cab of my truck. Stay. At least until you stop crying."

She wiped more tears from her cheeks. He stared at her. Not in a way that made her uncomfortable, but with concern. He wanted her to stay. Not for him, but for her. "What kind of dog do you have?"

"A golden retriever. Do you like dogs?"

She straddled the oak and lay with her back against the eroding bark. "I had a beagle growing up, until my sister Maura backed over him in the driveway."

"That's terrible. I'm sorry."

"It's okay. I think it was an accident."

"You *think* it was?"

"Probably. Anyway, I haven't been able to get close to a dog since."

"I'm sorry."

She shrugged. "It was a long time ago, nothing compared to what I deal with these days."

He reached for her and fingered a frizzy flyaway at her temple. Soon, two of his fingers massaged her scalp as he tucked the tendril away. She tensed initially, but soon sank into the comfort of his hand in her hair.

"Why don't you tell me why you think your husband's cheating on you?" He withdrew, leaving her both yearning for tender contact and relieved she wouldn't have to fight it.

She took a deep a breath. "He has an addictive personality. Nothing's ever enough—not a forty-hour work week, not one glass of whiskey."

"I'm sorry."

"Everything he does, he does in excess, be it entertaining his friends, or wagering obscene amounts at riverboat casinos. He may not be sleeping around—then again, what do I know? He's gone all the time—but he feeds his addictions instead of coming home to me. It's the same concept as buying a gift for another woman. On the surface, it's harmless, but a committed man simply should not do such things, am I right?"

He nodded. "I spend as much time as possible at home."

"My husband likes a good time. Three thousand dollars later, he's spent neither one minute nor one red cent on me, but I get to deal with the sloppy mess after the party."

She exhaled slowly. "I wish he were addicted to me."

CHAPTER 2

What had she been thinking, spending three hours alone in a forest preserve with Luke, airing her dirty laundry? She'd done less intelligent things, but not many. At nearly one o'clock—she was so late!—she stood in the shower at the club, too distracted to devise an excuse for her tardiness.

Oh, those hands, that smile. The craving between her legs. She had to see him again. *But how? When?* They could continue to meet at the club. *Just to talk.* Just to feel special together, assuming he felt as interested around her as she'd felt around him. *So special.*

But how would she explain her delay today? Brennan wouldn't believe she could exercise for three hours straight, and even if he would, he'd berate her for overdoing it during pregnancy. No, she needed an excuse, an alibi.

She went to the law library maybe? No, he'd only chastise her for pursuing the life she'd left behind.

She went shopping? *For what?* She didn't need anything.

She'd spent the past few hours at the Jasmine Vine, stuffing her face with whole-grain muffins? He'd buy that one, but she was still so hungry… Hungry for a married breastfeeding advocate she barely knew.

She'd lost her mind.

It was a harmless, albeit inappropriate, conversation. Her condition aside, Luke was married with two children. It wasn't as if he'd come on to her. But, with thoughts of his hand in her hair, a yearning surged within her, the likes of which she hadn't felt in years. His naked body belonged against hers, his mouth at her inner thigh, his hands wherever he damn well wanted to put them.

In two hours, five couples would file into her house. She didn't have time to contemplate grinding the handle of her bath brush deep between her legs, but the need, the desire, was too intense to ignore. His gorgeous mouth, with pouting lips and white, white teeth, and that darting pink tongue... Addicted, and she'd yet to taste a morsel of the sure-to-be tasty man.

Her clitoris swelled and tingled madly. She shirred her plump thighs together, stimulating the tender, private tissue just so. Would Luke watch a "pure and true" woman satisfy herself? Would he ask her to touch herself, request penetration, bury his fingers alongside hers?

She imagined him rolling her clit between his thick fingers, while his thumb probed her in rhythmic jabs, his tongue lapping against her nipples, sucking, biting.

The broad handle of her bath brush threatened to penetrate her, but, at the last second, she dropped it to the floor, unable to settle for plastic when she wanted the real thing. God, she'd give anything to make love with an attentive man, a man unafraid of spending his time with her, a man wanting badly to please her.

Out of breath and still in need of release, she leaned against the communal tile in the shower stall, forgetting for a moment about all the bodies that had pressed against it that morning. What was happening to her? Luke had innocently brushed a hair from her forehead, and suddenly, she needed his touch. Needed it the way she needed air to breathe.

Better to forget him before she was in over her head.

She turned off the water and wrapped herself in a bath towel from home. The club offered towel service, but Kimberley and women of her economic status always brought their own. The only guaranteed, freshly laundered linens were those Elsie folded in the upstairs laundry room.

She dressed at her locker.

Applied cosmetics at a less-than-pristine vanity.

Blow dried and styled her hair.

She dug through her cosmetics case for caramel apple nail polish, the perfect alibi. As a back-up plan, before her grant for college came through, she'd learned the art of manicuring. And she was good, better than most professionals. Until her belly swelled, she'd refuse to pay for nail treatment, but Brennan didn't have to know that.

* * *

"Dad?" Caleb used his aluminum bat like a cane, wandering toward the backstop at the park. "Are you leaving us again?"

Luke reached over Derby, who sauntered between them, and tapped his son's cap. "Why would you ask something like that?"

"Mom says it's just a matter of time before you go again." The bat clinked against the gravel once to two of Luke's heartbeats. "She says you're like your dad."

Clink, beat, beat. Clink, beat, beat reverberated in his ears. Anger seared in his gut like a chemical reaction in a test tube, but aside from the grinding of his teeth, he quickly hid it for his boy's sake. "Mom said that?"

"Is it true?"

"Let's get something straight." When he crouched beside him, Caleb stood above his eye level. He was growing taller every day. Time flew, and Luke knew, one day he'd wake up, and his eight-year-old would be earning a paycheck. As if Derby sensed a long discussion, he plopped to the ground and assumed his favorite sleeping position.

Caleb shifted toward Luke, kicking at dust. "Is it true?"

"I never leave you, got it?"

"Mom says when you leave her, you leave all of us."

Despite the humidity in the air, his throat felt dry, as if stuffed with cotton. He coughed and licked his lips, searching the horizon for the answer to this dilemma, but he knew no perfect words existed to soothe a child in constant fear of his parents' parting. "Is that what you think? You think I'd leave you?"

Caleb shrugged, tapping the bat into a patch of amber pea gravel. *Clink, clink, clink.* "You don't live at home anymore when you go."

"No, but not because I don't want to. Caleb..." Luke removed the bat from his son's grasp. It was impossible to think amid the noise. "Adults don't always agree on important things, Caleb. And when Mom and I don't agree, it's hard to live together, but I never leave *you*. I never want to live without you. I'm always going to be your dad, always going to be there."

"What about Rachael?"

From out of nowhere, sweat beaded on his upper lip, and he cleared his throat. "I'll always be her dad, too."

"Dad, do you love Mom?"

His legs, suddenly weak, shook when he rose. "Of course I love Mom."

"Does Mom love you?"

"Yeah." She wouldn't sleep with him, smile at him, or say one kind word to him, but deep down, she loved him, right? He'd always lived for that assumption, until the beautiful girl at the gym had twisted him in knots.

Kimberley had tensed when he raked through her hair, but almost instantly, she'd eased into comfort, as if she'd trusted him, as if she'd known him forever. He'd forgotten the thrill of an affectionate touch, of a woman's response to his hands. *So sweet.*

While he'd learned to live without it since Rachael Catherine had made her debut, he craved the buzz of reciprocal attention. And now, he couldn't shake the memory of this morning's source of it: Kimberley Roderick.

"Next time you leave, Dad, can I come with you?"

Luke clapped his hand against his thigh, alerting Derby. "Come on, boy."

"Can I?"

"I'm not going anywhere."

"Mom says you don't have time for kids without her help. She says your dad didn't take you, so you won't take me."

"Caleb, you want to know something about your grandpa?"

"Mom says you were Rachael's age when he left."

"Grandpa was a career military man. Do you know what that means? It means he moved from base to base, wherever our country needed him. He did it to protect your freedom."

"Why didn't you go with him? Why didn't Grandma?"

"Because adults don't always agree. Your grandpa's not a bad man." Just a lousy father, an even worse husband, and Luke would probably sucker-punch him in the jaw if he ever saw him again.

"You want me to go with you next time, don't you?"

"I always want you with me," Luke said, twisting his wedding ring. "Now stop worrying, kiddo." At the moment, he wanted to drop his wedding ring into Lake Michigan, Kimberley Roderick to a hotel room floor, and his divorce lawyer a line. "So, what do you say? Batting practice?"

"Coach says if I'm quicker with the grab, he might put me at shortstop this summer."

"Then we'll work on fielding. You'll make a good shortstop."

* * *

"Hi." Kimberley had one foot in the door when Brennan kissed the hollow of her neck, his breath a hot whiskey whisper at her throat. Hair of the dog that had devoured him last night. He closed the door and pressed her up against it. "Nails look great. Did you get a manicure?"

"And a pedicure." She hid her satisfied smile.

His fingers inched into her yoga pants. She recognized this pattern of behavior—he was sorry about last night, and he'd prove it with sex.

"Where's Allie?"

His tongue filled her mouth.

"Bren?" She turned her cheek to his demanding probe. "Where's Allie?"

"With my parents. They said they'd keep her all day." He spun her around and lowered her to the granite floor in the vestibule, his fingers working the zipper on her hooded sweatshirt.

"Here? Bren, we—"

"Sure we can."

She turned away, but that only enabled him to roll her over to her stomach and lift her hips to his pelvis. He pressed against her, rock hard. Overcharged from her taboo conversation with Luke, not to mention her near-masturbation in the shower, she groaned. Brennan's readiness sparked a passionate nerve, a needy desire to be stroked and penetrated. "Mmm." She pushed against his erection like a cat in heat, presenting.

"That's right. I know you like it like this." He peeled her pants down and shoved himself deeply into her. No time to undress, no time for foreplay, the fire between them urgent. But for all the wrong reasons. "God, you're dripping wet."

She imagined Luke behind her, gripping her waist and beating himself against her wet walls. Harder. Faster. When she pinched her eyes closed, Luke's large hands registered in her mind, caressing, doting, teasing.

It wouldn't always be this way, hard and unforgiving. Most of the time, she and Luke would probably make love leisurely, playfully, as if they had no place to be, nothing more important to do. They would talk about it for hours, tempting one another with lingering strokes and leering gazes in the forest preserve, before combusting behind closed doors.

He'd probably lick her first. A long drag of his moist tongue from her labia to her rectum, a thorough brushing around and inside her hole.

Get her good and wet, so his cock would slide in without effort, without nudging or coercion.

Unless, of course, he had prowess to surpass the average man. And with hands like his, he was probably well hung, with a circumference to come for. He'd want to work on her for hours with his fingers, his tongue. Oh, the thrill in making it fit, the teamwork involved in burying a well-endowed penis. Yet once in—all the way in—they'd move together naturally.

Pound into me. Deeper. Harder. It's not enough. I need more.

She tucked her hand into her panties and massaged her clit, the image of a perfect stranger interring himself soul-deep into her. Evocative eyes, straight teeth. Rugged smile.

You're a beautiful woman. Even Luke's voice exuded sex.

"That's it, that's it." Taut around the invasive cock, feeling every hard inch of it, she quivered. "That's it."

"Are you coming?" Brennan's voice.

Ignore it. Finish what you started.

"Are you coming, Kimmy?"

"Shh."

Deep, quick strokes into her slick vagina. And that was Luke slapping her ass, pushing into her, leading her over the edge. She rubbed with more precision.

"Are you coming?"

Yes.

"Let me look at you. I want to watch you come." He lifted one of her legs and in smooth movements, raised and rotated her body between plunges, racking her back against the stairs.

"Did you get there?"

Shut up.

A step lodged against the small of her back, and her orgasm broke. The digging of the stair treads against her back intensified the shattering of pleasure between her legs.

He cupped a breast, stroking her through her clothing. But now she'd come to her senses, she didn't need the incentive, and she didn't want him inside her. He wasn't the man she'd just come for. And the whiskey on his breath proved it.

* * *

Brennan placed a hand on her backside as she arranged cubes of cheese and sausage around a disc of baked *brie en croute* on a square platter. "Let's cater next time," he whispered. "This is too much for you."

"I enjoy it. Besides, hors d'oeuvres isn't exactly dinner for twelve. I can do this."

"We should try Coup de Gras. On Belmont."

"In the city? There's probably someone closer."

"Not as good."

City-boy mentality. Nothing was as good in the 'burbs as it was in the city.

"Lauren uses them, and her parties are always lavishly supplied, Kimmy, don't you think?"

Kimberley might have been offended that Brennan compared her cooking to his ex-girlfriend's caterer's, but Lauren Wagner had been her best friend for years. "Very elegant, yes. Expensive, too, I'm sure."

"You're too frugal when it comes to this stuff." He slid his arms around her, drumming his fingers against her abdomen, and snuggling behind her. "Have you thought about how we're going to handle this tonight?"

"You mean whether we should tell people about the pregnancy?"

"Yeah…what do you think?"

She'd been too busy thinking about Luke to ponder the breaking of their news, wondering if the physically fit stranger was as good in bed as he looked, as phenomenal as he'd been in her mind against the stairs.

"Maybe you can nurse a glass of red wine all night. Then no one will be suspicious."

A sigh, half desperation, half disappointment, escaped her. "Brennan, I love you."

His arms tightened around her. "I love you, too."

"But I'm not going to allow our children to grow up thinking every big event in life demands a lavish dent in the pocket book, or—"

"There's nothing wrong with paying for a service."

"—or involves over-consumption."

He pressed his forehead against her shoulder. "Do we have to talk about it every god-damned night? I've been looking forward to this party all week. It's the highlight in my week of fast food and hotel curtains, and all you want to talk about is—"

The front doorbell sounded and he backed away, tapping her on the backside.

"I'll get the door," she said, wiping her hands on a tea towel and walking to the front of the house.

"Honey, you're pregnant." Lauren hadn't taken off her jacket or moved beyond the foyer. Her big, blue eyes seemed to grow even larger with excitement, and her pretty pink lips puckered.

Kimberley attempted to deny the inference with a shake of her head, but it was no use. "You're scaring me."

"Sixth sense about pregnancy. Am I right?"

"Don't tell anyone."

"Such great news." Lauren turned a make-believe key at her lips and with the flick of her white-blonde hair, tossed said key over her shoulder. Magical and magnetic, she drew fans the way a queen bee attracted soldiers.

And she'd do anything for a friend. Need a babysitter? At midnight? Lauren's your girl. Need a new tailor? Lauren knew the right guy. Need an extra bridesmaid? Kimberley did, and Lauren filled in with more enthusiasm than either of Kimberley's sisters. So it was only fitting she knew the Rodericks' secret.

The lilac satin pumps on Lauren's feet—remnants from a wedding years ago—coordinated with the handbag dangling from her tiny wrist. "Pregnant with number two. Can I congratulate Bren?"

"He knows, if that's what you're asking."

"Well, how do I know?" She pulled a chic, silver jacket from her shoulders to reveal the sexiest garment any mother of four had ever donned: a shimmering ivory catsuit—vinyl—with a halter-style top. "He's been out of town more than he's been in. For all I know, you haven't had time to kiss him hello."

Kimberley pressed a hand to her bruised back and glanced at the staircase. "Oh, we've accomplished that."

With a bottle of No.7 whiskey and bunch of spring flowers, Lauren's husband Rick approached the house, pocketing his cell phone. "I know something you don't know," Lauren sang.

"All right." Kimberley took the bottle and bouquet from Rick. "You can tell him."

"They're pregnant." Lauren grasped her husband's hands and leaned to kiss him. "They're catching up. But don't tell anyone."

"Congratulations, buddy." Rick looked directly over Kimberley's head at Brennan, who moved toward them with his hands shoved into his pockets. "You're halfway to four."

"I think this is our last," Kimberley said. "I want to go back to work someday."

Lauren waved the thought away. "Whatever for?"

Brennan hooked an arm around her waist. A little too tight. "I see we've decided to share our news."

"Don't blame her," Lauren said. "I guessed."

"This calls for a celebratory shot, don't you think?" Rick said.

After a hesitant glance into Kimberley's eyes, Brennan nodded. "Why stop at one?"

She felt her heart sinking.

"Who do you like in the Cubs-Astros series?" Brennan asked. "Care to make it interesting?"

* * *

"Don't even think about it," Diane said in the darkness, rolling out from under Luke's hands to the edge of the mattress.

"Diane," he whispered, inching closer. "Please."

"You want me to spread my legs so you can hop up and down on me until you're satisfied?"

"No, I want—"

"Here." She spread her limbs, lying in an X. "Go."

"I want you to enjoy it, too." He leaned over her, daring to weave a hand into her brassy hair. If not for the look of contempt in her ice blue eyes, she'd be the same girl he fell for so long ago. There had been a time when that fire had nothing to do with anger, but verve. The ancient image of her reaching orgasm ricocheted inside him like a pinball. "I want you to want me. The way you used to."

"I have never enjoyed it with you." Her sharp glare might as well have been a shard of glass, ripping through his heart. "I can't stand the sight of you, much less the feel of you."

He turned his back to her, punching the pillow into submission before settling into it. "This isn't right. It isn't natural."

"If you have to have it, find yourself a little friend and leave me out of your natural urges. Fuck every fucking whore in town until your dick falls off."

"I don't want that, and you know it."

A staccato, snake-like laugh hissed from her lips. "Given the chance, you'd be screwing everything you could get your dirty hands on. In bar bathrooms, backseats, sleazy motels."

"I love you."

"Right."

"Why won't you let me love you?"

After a long, drawn out exhalation, she gave her head a tiny shake.

"I had a talk with Caleb today."

"About what?" He turned toward her again and dropped a hand onto her stomach; surprisingly, she allowed it to remain there after only a tremor of distaste.

"Where the hell do you get off telling him you're taking him with you next time you leave, Luke?"

"I didn't—"

"I carried him. I threw up for ten weeks. I got stretch marks on my ass, I went through fourteen hours of labor, and I spent three hours pushing him out of my body. What makes you think he's yours to take?"

"First, I was right there with you, through it all."

"Doing nothing next to what I did."

"Doing what I could. And second, he's not the last piece of pizza, he's our son. And I didn't—"

"You don't even know how to open a can of Spaghetti-O's. What makes you think you can be a single father?"

"Let me love you, Diane. I don't want to be a single father. I want us to be happy again."

She shook her head.

His hand traveled to her sexless cotton briefs, and although she sighed in boredom, she allowed him access. "Diane." He slowly and gently pressed a finger into her folds, searching for the one spot that used to do the trick. He hadn't come close to finding it in years. "Try to enjoy it."

She lay like a limp rag doll, completely unresponsive. Biologically, she felt right. Warm and moist on the inside. But on the outside, stiff and uninterested.

"Just get it over with," she said. "I'd like to get some sleep tonight."

He pulled his hands from her underwear. *No, thanks.*

"Fine." She yanked the sheets over her body and rolled away. "But for the record, I was willing. You make the concession next time."

He rolled out of bed, tucked his rigid cock back into his boxer shorts, and pulled on a pair of jeans and a flannel.

"Take that damn dog with you, wherever you're going."

"Of course."

"But those children are mine."

He fastened the last button and darted out of the bedroom. Derby fell into place beside him, and to accommodate the dog's leisurely saunter, Luke slowed his pace. "It's all right, Derby. We'll make it through."

The stairs might as well have been Mount Everest for the pup. Too old to make the climb, he often slept by the back door instead of outside the master bedroom, where he'd been this night. Luke lifted the dog's weight and carried him down. "You're heavy."

Derby groaned in sympathetic, brotherhood fashion, his sad eyes blinking slowly, as if he knew of the rejection behind closed doors. And maybe he did. The Discovery Channel had played a documentary on companionship last month, confirming what Luke had already suspected: Derby felt pain when his master was sad and elation when Luke was happy. Studies had shown that just as long-term spouses often died within weeks of one another, pets of the elderly had done the same.

"You and me, pup. We got to stick together."

They stopped in Luke's tiny den. It once was a breezeway connecting their smallish house to the garage, but when Luke had gone into business for himself a few years ago, he'd enclosed it. It was far from ideal. Diane traipsed through with groceries and laundry, and the kids were constantly in and out. Case in point, he tossed the half-eaten apple screaming *Rachael was here* into the trash. But it was a sufficient place to keep his sister's old computer.

Derby sprawled like a red-gold spill on the beaten peel-and-stick vinyl, while Luke waited for a connection to the Internet. Diane probably thought he surfed for one of those seedy sex sites to relieve the pressure in his pants. In truth, he'd rather she hold onto that belief than know what he was really doing.

People search. Kimberley Roderick. Brennan Roderick. He tried variations of spellings, but nothing came up in the north suburbs. For ten dollars, he could receive a full report on the unlisted Brennan Roderick, complete with address, phone number, and e-mail, if he had it, which he probably did. Corporate types like Kimberley's husband checked e-mail several times an hour.

Luke could spare ten dollars, but he couldn't afford Diane's opening the information, and they shared an e-mail account. He'd have to find that beautiful, passionate girl another way.

Derby lifted his chin, accusingly.

"I just want to know she's okay, boy." Well, all right, that wasn't all he wanted, but he'd settle for only a smile.

And what a pretty smile it was, lighting up her eyes like Christmas on State Street.

* * *

"I swear to God," Lauren said, holding her right hand up in testimonial fashion. "I just told the woman there was no way I was paying full price for a dress already on the sale rack, and she knocked twenty-two dollars off. No questions asked." She shrugged and sipped her water.

"You should have a look at that new boutique on Ashton, Kimberley. Not that you'll be showing by the dinner cruise, but you might find something for the holidays."

Kimberley tried to smile, although she hated shopping in the city. "I'll keep that in mind."

"Great prices," Lauren said, "and they haggle."

The male guests seated at the Rodericks' recreation room bar raised their glasses, toasting Kimberley's pregnancy for the twentieth time, while the females exchanged bargain stories of maternity clothes shopping. Exhausting, but partly amusing, seeing not one woman present needed to save twenty-two dollars.

Kimberley glanced around her circle of friends. Amongst her sat former cheerleaders, homecoming queens, and one former Miss Cook County.

Gina, six months pregnant with child number four, looked better than the day she won her crown.

Marilyn's figure tempted Kimberley to turn bulimic.

Jennifer's husband couldn't stop looking at her, no matter how far across the room he was stationed.

Christine, ready to deliver her fourth baby in five-and-a-half years, never ceased to smile, although her tiny ankles were encircled by the straps of sexy, two-inch-heel pumps.

And Lauren, the absolute doll Brennan had once loved.

While these beauty queens had nestled in their over-priced, three-flat apartments, cooking dinner for their just-out-of-college husbands, or at the very least phoning caterers, Kimberley had been studying in the most prestigious law libraries in this country. While these Polly Annas memorized their ovulation cycles, Kimberley had aced the bar exams.

But the wedding rings and hordes of children didn't fool Kimberley. These were traditional Lincoln Park Trixies, married to Chicago's metrosexuals. The most popular girls in town, most likely snickering at lowly Kimberley, hailing from a broken home in Lake Villa, Illinois.

"So this prospective hire and I had lunch last week in Atlantic

City," Brennan said to Rick.

Kimberley's ears perked up. Eavesdropping was the only way she learned of happenings out-of-town.

"He turned down the job," Brennan continued. "Wants to be home with his family. Can you imagine that? Passing up this kind of coin for a warm bed seven nights a week? If he's that antsy, you'd think he'd find another...outlet, shall we say? I tell you, sending him out on the road would do his wife a favor, teach her to appreciate the time they do have. And if she doesn't, family-shmamily. She'd be there to clean up on pay day, I promise you."

"I'm going to bed," Kimberley whispered to Lauren.

The need to escape this charade had suddenly overwhelmed her. Brennan's hand, holding a highball glass of whiskey, worked independently of his mind. Lift the glass to the lips. Swallow. Repeat. Refill. And she wasn't supposed to notice, wasn't supposed to care her husband uttered things like 'family-schmamily,' so long as he kept her amply clothed and fed, locked in a nice house, which might as well have been a pumpkin shell.

"Honey, he's drunk." Lauren pressed Kimberley's hand against the bar. "He doesn't mean any of that."

"Alcohol is truth serum. And I'm tired." Tired physically, tired emotionally. Tired of standing behind his addictions and watching her husband flaunt his money, as if it were a measure of his worth.

"It isn't even ten o'clock yet."

"Long day." She swiveled the barstool, and leapt to the floor.

"Want some company, honey?"

"No thanks, Lauren."

"I've been there, remember?" She eyed her, knowingly. "Give me a call tomorrow, all right?"

"Sure."

"Kimmy, wait." Brennan grasped Kimberley's hand from his position behind the bar and delayed his conversation with Rick long enough to say, "Don't go."

His blue eyes blazed, reminding her that she'd married an intelligent, good-looking, and charming man. But he'd surrendered to many addictions long before they'd met.

"I'm exhausted," she said, attempting a smile.

"We're hosting." Brennan chucked her under the chin, as if she were a little girl. "How do you think it looks when my wife leaves my party early?"

"Like she's tired."

"I want a partner in this."

Bullshit... He wanted an ornament. "We aren't partners in anything anymore."

"Watch your tone."

She refrained from screaming and instead took a deep breath. "Good night."

On her way up to bed, she stopped in the kitchen for *The Fabulous Gourmet*, ready to delve into the reverence long ago showered upon her. But once cradled in expensive linens in her marital bed, her fingers following Jason's script, she imagined Luke's voice reciting the age-old words scripted on the paper. She closed her eyes, hearing him, smelling him, feeling his hands in her hair.

"Why do you care about me?" she whispered, concentrating on the memory of his touch. "And, my God, why do I want you to?"

CHAPTER 3

Yes, she'd lost her mind.

A hung-over husband and a child at the in-laws' gave Kimberley some free time. She spent it in the parking lot at Gallant's Gym, waiting for Luke, praying for his "usual" Sunday run.

Should she happen to see him, she probably wouldn't utter a word, but oh, to look at him. Just for a moment or two. Like a schoolgirl with a crush on a popular boy, she knew she couldn't have him, but who could resist the urge to dream?

What would he do, if he saw her there? Would he be pleased, flash that brilliant smile? Or would he sprint in the other direction to avoid the crazy, pregnant lady who'd gotten the wrong idea?

Oh, leave before you embarrass yourself.

But she wanted to stare at his beautiful body, into those gorgeous, caring eyes.

Go, go, go. Now.

She turned the key in the ignition and exhaled. Done. Doing well, making progress. She glanced in the rearview mirror and looked to the left side mirror. "Oh, my God!"

"Hey, beautiful girl." Luke stood a few inches from the open window, rubbing a callus on his palm, just below his wedding band.

"You scared me."

"Mind if I get in?"

Her jaw began to descend, and she shook her head. "No."

"I'm harmless." He twisted his ring.

"I meant no, as in I don't mind."

"Good." With a smile wide enough to crinkle that mysterious scar at his eye, he walked around the vehicle, opened the door, and sank into the passenger seat. "So…"

"So, what?"

"Rough night?"

"You could say that."

"Did you work out this morning? Diane's doctor suggests exercising only every other day during pregnancy. Be careful, all right?"

"Do I look like I just spent an hour on a yoga mat?"

"No, actually, you don't. Great lipstick."

Lipstick? Oh, yes, Ruby Tuesday. "Thanks."

"Let's get out of here."

"I beg your pardon?"

"I said, let's go."

"Go where?"

"I don't know. Anywhere." He shrugged. "Are you hungry? There's a little sandwich shop off the beaten path between here and Des Plaines."

"I don't know…"

"What? Did you have something else in mind?"

She palmed the steering wheel, as if the leather were Luke's irresistible chest. It had been too long since she'd trailed her hands over a muscled frame. Counting the ridges in Jason's abs had been one of her favorite pastimes, and Luke's probably surpassed Jason's by a hundred. "Do you think we should be seen together?"

He raised a brow. "Do you think we shouldn't?"

Heat filtered into her cheeks.

"Well, thank you," he said. "That's flattering."

Too nervous to say anything in return, she swallowed hard and waited for him to speak again. A lawyer's trick: witnesses with loose tongues filled unbearable silences.

"Take a left," he said. "No one will see us in this hole in the wall, I assure you."

She began to drive.

"So," he said. "Seedy motel? Or are you hungry?"

"I'm pretty hungry." Although she pretended not to hear his prior suggestion, a mad sensation darted between her legs. To lock herself in some flea-bag with this fine specimen of testosterone…there was no telling what she might do.

"I had a rough night myself." He grasped her hand. "But why don't you tell me about yours?"

"Same thing that happens every Saturday night."

His thumb traveled over her knuckles. "He was drunk."

"Yes."

"And he lost money."

"A little bit, yeah."

"Did he..." Luke shook his head. "Never mind."

"Did he what?"

"I was going to ask if he hurt you, but how crazy is that?"

Perhaps if Brennan had physically hurt her last night, she'd have an excuse to leave, and no one would blame her for wanting to.

"I wouldn't mind rescuing you, but you shouldn't stay with a guy who hit you."

Would she? Abuse was abuse, and Brennan's intoxicated activities certainly fit into the same category. Would a weekly pounding be any different? Too much a parallel to consider at the moment. "What about you? What happened to you last night?"

"Same thing that happens every Saturday night." He chuckled and squeezed her hand. "Next road, turn right. After two stop signs, there's a tiny, blink-and-you'll-miss-it lane on the right. Take it and follow it to Neverland."

She turned onto a practically hidden road, dotted with potholes. "Luke, can I have my hand back?"

"No."

"No?"

"I haven't held hands with someone in...well, years. And it's a noncommittal gesture. Ever hear of Hands Across America? Those people were strangers. We're practically old friends compared to them."

His hand comforted hers like a vague memory. Such simple contact, but warm, consoling, and a rare validation that she was worthy of tender attention.

His hand in her hair had seemed much more suggestive than this, but holding hands could only be considered innocent at age fourteen. Being married with children and charged like an electron, holding Luke's hand was a prelude to sex, either mental, or heaven help her, physical.

I shouldn't. I just shouldn't. She gently resisted his hold, but when he tightened his grip, she surrendered far too quickly.

Only when she needed to parallel park the car in front of an ancient storefront, nearly fifteen minutes later, did he release her hand.

The rickety stairs creaked when they climbed, and the wooden siding was shedding flakes of pink Victorian paint. The faded sign on the door, "Sandwich Shop," warmed her heart with memories of another neglected inn of her past. *Dot's Diner. Lake Villa. Jason.*

Luke took her hand and opened the door.

"We're in public," she said, attempting to pull away. "Not a good idea."

"Please. Let me be the envy of the two grandpas at the corner table."

"I'm married."

His eyes pleaded. "It's all make-believe off the beaten path, beautiful girl," he whispered. "Let's pretend."

Could it hurt? Who would see her in this crumbling structure, in a town Brennan and his friends wouldn't tiptoe through? With tentative fingers, she touched his hand, and they entered the sandwich shop.

The occupants' eyes lingered upon them. An old man nodded. "Cute couple of kids."

They sat at a cozy table for two, and within moments, a woman approached, late forties, clad in a pink apron and a silver nametag—Rosa—with a notepad. "What would you like?" Her gum popped.

Kimberley scanned the tabletop for a menu and found none. "What do you have?"

Rosa scratched her head with the eraser end of a short pencil. "Sandwiches. You name the combo."

Across the table, Luke stroked her hand with his thumb and looked to the waitress. "Roast beef, turkey, and Swiss on a roll. And for my wife, chicken and cheddar on wheat. She's pregnant and needs the extra grains."

"Will do." Rosa popped her gum again. "Hot or cold?"

"Hot," they said together.

With a nod, the waitress turned her back.

"Hope that's all right," he whispered.

"I'm not choosy. I'll eat just about anything."

"No, that I called you my wife."

Heat crept to her cheeks. "It's all make-believe."

They ate in comfortable silence, occasionally breaking contact, but returning to their adjoined position whenever possible.

When the check arrived, Kimberley picked it up.

"Let me get it," he said.

"If my husband's going to bet two hundred dollars against the Cubs, I can spare ten for lunch."

He shrugged and helped himself to one of the red-and-white striped mints, which had accompanied the tab. "Then you'll have to go out with me again sometime. So I can return the favor."

She felt a smile coming on. "We'll see."

Once they settled into the car, he again took her hand, and they rode in comfortable silence back toward Gallant's.

"So," he finally said. "Quite a coincidence, our seeing each other today."

"Yes, it was."

He smiled, leaning back in his seat. "Yeah, same thing as every Saturday night."

He didn't elaborate, and Kimberley didn't probe. Neither said another word until he stepped out of her car in the parking lot.

"Thanks for lunch," he said, leaning on her door, resting his elbows on the open window.

"You're welcome."

"So maybe I'll see you around, Kimber."

What an exotic, dreamy twist to her name. So much more sophisticated than Kimmy. "Maybe."

He winked and turned away.

* * *

A few days later, therapist Ben Schaeffer stared at Luke over wire-rimmed glasses. "What would you say is the biggest problem in your marriage?"

Just out of college, Luke figured Benny probably worked for beans for Cook County. What did he know about life, let alone marriage?

This would have been Luke's tenth session, had he not blown off his ninth for Ms. Kimberley Quinn Roderick last Saturday. That's right, he knew her middle name now. Amazing what a Gallant's Gym towel boy had been willing to look up for twenty bucks.

Luke glanced at the empty chair to his right, where Diane would have been sitting, if she gave a damn. "The biggest problem in my marriage," he said. "The whole damn thing's a problem, if you ask me."

"Break it down for me."

Systematically, he ground his teeth together. *Keep your eye on the prize: Caleb and Rachael.* "You want the biggest issue."

"That's right," Schaeffer said. "The biggest obstacle."

"Aside from the fact I claim a daughter who isn't mine, work my fingers to the bone and don't make enough money to keep my wife happy, and I have the best golden retriever on the planet and she hates him?"

"Her contempt for your dog is one of your biggest problems?"

"She won't even walk him. Everything that might help me is an inconvenience for her. She doesn't do anything for me."

Schaeffer raised his thin eyebrows. "She does nothing?"

"I work, I bring home checks, and she cashes them."

"You said last week she's in charge of your finances."

"She is, but that's her only job."

"You don't think raising two children and keeping the house are jobs worth mentioning?"

Luke shook his head in resignation. "Look, I know what she does is important. But there's more to a marriage than ironed shirts and hot dinners, you know? It's the whole package, not just her keeping score. The only reason she keeps my house is so she can martyr herself for doing so."

"What else is important to you, in regards to your marriage, Mr. Jackson?"

"Call me Luke."

Dr. Schaeffer nodded. "I prefer to keep things formal, Mr. Jackson. What else is important to—"

"Intimacy."

Schaeffer fingered his closely shaven chin, assuming he was old enough to shave. "Go on."

"Two or three times a year. That's what I've been living with since my boy was born. She doesn't do anything for me."

Schaeffer nodded silently.

"And it isn't my fault. I'm willing to take my time with her, to help her out, if you know what I mean. I'm not selfish in bed, but after eight years of hurry-up sex, it's obvious she doesn't want anything from me. Wouldn't you want to do it as quickly as possible? To make sure you have time to finish?"

Schaeffer took a breath, as if he didn't know what to say. Maybe he had no frame of reference. He was probably a virgin. Who'd have him?

"She hates sex," Luke said. "Well, she hates it with me anyway."

Schaeffer didn't flinch. "Have you thought about the fact she hates it"—His fingers became visual quotation marks—"and still does it for you?"

Across a battered coffee table, Luke stared, fighting the lava threatening to erupt inside him. "I don't force myself on my wife. I care about Diane's feelings."

"Do you?"

"What do you know? Are you there when I try to touch her? I'd spend hours with my tongue between her legs, if she'd allow it. But if I stroke her, kiss her, try to love her at all, she pulls away. Is that—having sex with me twice a year—doing it for me?" He rose from his seat and turned toward the door.

"There are forty-three minutes left of this session, Mr. Jackson."

"Yeah, yeah. Enough time for fourteen sexual encounters with my wife, and one minute to spare for clean-up. I've done the math more than I care to admit."

"We're not done, Mr. Jackson."

"I am."

"Same time Saturday then."

Although the thought of one more moment in-session with this snot-nose, know-it-all kid made him want to regurgitate his breakfast, Luke nodded. Without looking back, he rushed through the waiting room, through the county counseling wing, and through the parking lot, chilly rain pounding down upon his head.

Derby groaned when Luke unlocked and opened the driver-side truck door. The warm air inside greeted him, thawed him the way he imagined Kimberley Roderick might after a cold night plowing driveways.

The old picture pressed into the dashboard—he and Diane with their son on his second birthday—caught his eye, and he scrutinized the photo for the millionth time, searching for a clue Diane had been lost to him even then. But not a hint existed. Not then, and not now. Paul Radcliffe had been pleasuring his wife a few times a week back then, and for all he knew, the bastard could be servicing her again now.

"Come on, Derby. Let's pick up the kids from school."

*   *   *

Brennan arrived home on schedule, at three o'clock Friday afternoon, his arm outstretched to a screeching Allison. "Daddy, Daddy!"

Kimberley remained glued to her seat in the breakfast room, nursing a mug of decaffeinated tea. With an ex-boyfriend perpetually milling around in her mind, she shouldn't have room to think about the stranger fond of holding hands, but the energy Luke evoked raced through her veins like lightning through a summer sky. "Doesn't Mommy look nice today?" Brennan approached the breakfast table. His gorgeous blue eyes sparkled, fixated on Kimberley. "But Mommy looks nice every day, doesn't she?"

Preoccupied with the father too hung over to play with her last weekend, Allison's attention remained focused on him, her little hands rubbing his five o'clock shadow.

"Let's give Mommy a kiss together." He kissed one cheek, and Allison's chatter stopped just long enough for her to peck the other.

"Down, Daddy. Want to play?" She wiggled her way to the floor and scampered to her dolls.

"I'm sorry," Brennan whispered, gingerly tousling her hair. "About last weekend, about everything, Kim."

She pressed her lips together and met his gaze. "Do you love me?"

"What kind of a question is that?"

A lone tear escaped, but she caught it on the tip of her little finger. "Yes or no."

"You know I do."

"I don't feel loved."

"Don't say that." His arms enveloped her. "I don't want to make you feel that way."

"How do you expect me to feel when you do what you do? Brennan, we've been together eight years, and you're obviously—"

"I'll try harder."

"I'm tired of hearing that. Things have to change."

"It all comes out in the wash, Kimmy. So I lost a few hundred to Rick. He'll lose it back to me next week." He grinned. "Luck is on my side. I found you, didn't I?"

"I'm more concerned with what happens after the betting than your luck. You have an addictive personality, and you can't get enough. Of anything."

"I can't get enough of you, that's for sure." His hand grazed up her side. Just before he cupped her breast, she flinched away.

"Think about the tiny audience five feet away, and please, think about what I said. You need help."

"It's taken a good many years for me to make the progress I've made, and it'll take a good many more before we're done. I used to be at the track every night, in Vegas at least once a month." He kissed the top of her head. "I'm trying, Kim. Don't you know I'll never stop trying? Believe me. Please."

She pressed a hand to her abdomen and observed Allison's play. "I don't have a choice."

CHAPTER 4

"Hey, beautiful girl." Luke approached the stepping machines, cracking a smile. A bicep threatened to rip his cotton T-shirt. The man needed new shirts. Desperately.

Kimberley skimmed her fingers over a tiny rip near his collar bone. He was hot to the touch. And firm. Hard. Their gazes met, and she snapped her hand away. "Your shirt's torn."

"Yeah." He stepped onto the machine next to hers. "So...have you talked to your husband about breastfeeding?"

Frowning, she helped herself to a sip of his water. "Do you work for a breastfeeding advocacy group?"

"No." His ultra-white teeth gleamed. "I just think it's important. Besides, I need to know if I should be jealous."

"I beg your pardon?"

"I'd be jealous of anyone who got any of those."

"Would you compliment them in their usual, barely-B state? Let me guess. Your wife is a standard-D."

"No."

"Bigger?"

"You really want to talk about my wife's breasts?"

"No." Despite the guy's inept flirting, which was charming as hell, he probably knew his way around the female breast well enough to guide a tour. Those hands, that mouth... An undeniable urge to climax, right then and there, flushed through her.

"Your husband's a lucky guy."

"No, he isn't."

"Yes, he is."

"No, he isn't. Men forever covet what they do not have, but that never made my husband lucky, or Jason, for that matter. Given the chance, you think you'd be lucky, too, but you'd be sorely mistaken."

"Who's Jason?"

She shifted her glance to the monitor on the stepper. "No one."

After a few silent seconds, Luke piped up. "You know, this planet wants the strongest and most beautiful of a species to procreate."

"What?"

"It's true. I saw it on the Discovery Channel. If you watch two sperm from two different men under a microscope, the stronger of the two will attack. It's scientific. It's nature's way. Men protect what's rightfully theirs, and if you were rightfully mine, I'd be the luckiest guy in the world."

A delightful burst of pleasure surged between her legs.

"I'll bet a hundred-to-one my soldiers would bury your husband's swimmers in a second. You're far too pretty for him, I'm sure of it. So tell me. Do you cheat on your husband?"

"What? No!" Then again, she'd heard Brennan's family-shmamily.

"So Jason's an old flame." Luke's brown eyes narrowed, and he brushed a thumb over the moon-shaped scar near his eye.

"Married four years ago come September to an hourglass figure with gorgeous blonde hair."

"Diane's my high school sweetheart. I don't have any ex-girlfriends."

"Oh, come on. Men like you play the field in excess."

"Well, I have ex-lovers, just not ex-girlfriends. I did my share of chasing skirts in the army."

Great. An ex-soldier. Loves his children, loves his country. Watch me melt.

"Don't think less of me for it," he said. "Sex is necessary for survival, you know, and when you're faced with a real possibility of dying...well, animal instinct takes over. Kind of wish you were around when it did. Then that baby might be mine."

Had Luke ever pounded into his wife, or any of his ex-lovers, on the stairs? Would he ever pound into her? She stopped stepping, mouth agape, brow knit. What had she gotten herself into? She stepped off the apparatus and wiped her towel across her forehead. "I'm not going to cheat on my husband with you."

Luke flashed his killer smile and joined her on a walk toward the locker room. "Who would you cheat on your husband with? Jason?"

"In my mind, I already have. But that's as far as it goes."

"Did you cry when he got married?"

She stopped walking and turned toward him. "Why does that matter?"

"Just curious." His gaze remained planted on her eyes, but a sexual aura surrounded his body.

Oh, to feel those hands trailing along her skin, cupping her breasts, raking through her hair.

"Do you want to cheat on your wife with me?" God, that sounded like an invitation.

"Yes."

"I'm pregnant."

"I didn't say I'd let it happen. You asked a question, and I answered truthfully. Yes, Kimberley, I'd love to make love to you, but no, it'll never happen. I'm married." He twisted his wedding band. "And my kids mean everything to me."

Dumbstruck, she shook her head, hoping for a few words to fall to her tongue.

"I thought we were pretty clear on that," Luke said.

"Clarity. There's a pipe dream for you." She stared at a poster on the wall. Believe it. Become it, it said. "For three hours. I cried for three hours in a tepid bubble bath one week before Jason got married."

"Because he replaced you with the hourglass?"

"Because he loved me once. And now, he doesn't know me. And he doesn't care."

Luke rested a hand on her abdomen. When she was pregnant with Allison, she hated people touching her belly, but Luke's hand melded against her body as if it belonged there.

"He was a fool to leave you, Kimberley."

"He wasn't a fool. He was young. And so was I."

"He was a fool." His strong hand massaged her stomach, and she leaned into him, praying for his hand to slip. Up or down, she didn't care, but she needed to feel his touch in areas much more intimate than her tummy.

Her cheeks flushing hot, she caught her breath and stepped away. "I have to go. Brennan and I are going out tonight, and I have a hundred things to do."

Luke nodded. "He was a fool, Kimberley."

"I have to go." Dazed, she backed away, hurried into the locker room, gathered her things, and headed to the market.

* * *

"I'm going to cheat on my wife." There. He'd said it.

Schaeffer pressed his fingers together in a rigid tee-pee. For a moment, he appeared peaked, flustered. "You're going to…to…what?"

"I met someone, Doc. And I think she needs me as much I need her."

The pipsqueak cleared his throat. "Do you…do you think sexual gratification with this woman will replace the mental intimacy you share with your wife?"

Luke forfeited his good posture and stretched the entire length of his body in the uncomfortable chair, his feet honing in on the space under the coffee table. "A: there's nothing intimate left between Diane and me. And B: yeah."

"Let's talk about the consequences, Mr. Jackson."

"All right. And it's Luke, by the way."

"Consequence number one. Losing your wife."

"I already lost her to Paul Radcliffe six years ago."

"Paul…who?"

"Keep up with me, Benny." Luke clasped his hands behind his head. "Paul Radcliffe. Rachael's biological father."

"It's Doctor Schaeffer. Please."

"I take issue with that. If we're going to discuss my darkest, secret desires, I'd rather be on a first-name basis."

"The formality of a title keeps our relationship professional. Don't think of me as a bartender. Think of me as your therapist."

"And I can't do that and call you Ben?"

"We're getting away from the issue at hand. You assume Mr. Radcliffe is Rachael's father. Why?"

"Because I've never known a baby to grow *in utero* for an entire year, that's why."

"Have you performed DNA tests to prove she isn't yours?"

"There's no reason to. When Diane told me she was pregnant, she knew I'd leave. She already had my bag packed. I'm no mathematical genius, but—"

"Your name is on the birth certificate."

"Yes."

"Rachael shares your last name."

"Yes."

"You love her as if she's your own."

"Absolutely."

"Then why are you using Diane's past infidelity—one you've obviously accepted—as an excuse to cheat on your wife?"

He took a deep breath. "I'm not using it at all. I don't need an excuse, and I don't need a reason. All I need is the desire, and trust me, I've got that one covered."

"Let's talk more about Rachael, about why you raise her as your own."

"She's a little girl. None of this is her fault."

"So it has nothing to do with keeping Diane."

"No, it's about the well-being of my daughter, and the confidence and character of my son." He straightened to a ramrod position. "Everything I do, I do for them, with them in mind. I'm not using them to keep my wife around."

"So when you decided to have an affair, you did so with your children in mind?"

Luke rubbed at a callus on his thumb, looking the doctor in the eye. "Listen. I'm not a bad guy."

"I'm not judging you."

"The hell you're not."

"You're here for marriage counseling. You tell me you're going to have an affair. It's my job to help you think this through before you—"

"I've already thought it through."

"Then why are you here? I have plenty of clients who want my help. You're not one of them."

"You want to know what I want? I want you to tell me how to eke by in this marriage for the next thirteen years, so I can keep my kids under the same roof. With me, and yes, with my dog. I'm not looking for some magic formula to make Diane and me what we used to be. We're long gone, probably dead before I left for Saudi, and we're never coming back."

"Again, if that's the case, why are you here?"

"Because I can't live without my children, and that means I have to live with Diane. I'm just looking for a strategy to make that possible."

Schaeffer shuffled through some papers on the coffee table. "All right, a few weeks ago, you mentioned you're closer with your son—Colin, is it?—than with your daughter."

"Caleb. And that's right."

"Caleb?"

"It's Biblical. Caleb led his generation into the promised land once his elders were banished for lost faith."

Catching the parallel, Dr. Schaeffer coughed. "Oh."

* * *

"Oh, hello, 3-4-3-7."

Kimberley's drycleaner, Asian and petite, smiled. A year ago, she couldn't speak a word of English, but she now referred to Kimberley by the last four digits of her phone number. Mr. Drycleaner ironed with the full-shirt press twenty feet away, and she barked a string of Korean words, too harsh to come out of such a minute body, to alert him. He scrambled to retrieve the clothes. She turned back to Kimberley with a smile. "How you today, 3-4-3-7?"

"I'm well, thanks." Kimberley handed over her claim ticket. "How do you remember all those phone numbers?"

"Oh, you beautiful lady. I not remember all customer, just pretty one."

"Thank you." Kimberley drummed her fingers against her abdomen, searching for the warmth of Luke's caress, left behind at the gym.

"I not a lesbian, but you beautiful. Easy remember." The drycleaner's smile vanished, and she screamed a few hundred syllables at Mr. Drycleaner, who, with a broad smile, clipped the bagged order onto a rod, ignoring his wife's rant. All peaches and cream again, she turned back to Kimberley. "Ten shirt and seven pant. Your husband go work naked? I have all clothes."

"No, he's a shopper. He has more to wear than I do."

"Oh, that good. Husband shop, buy present. Happy wife, no?"

If only it were that simple. "Absolutely. He's taking me to dinner tonight."

"Oh, lucky lady."

She fished through her purse for her credit card, stumbling across the head of UIC's History Department's business card. *Might as well toss it in the trash. Lucky, right.* So lucky her life no longer belonged to her.

But an hour ago, she'd felt as if she were rolling in clover. Luke. The imprint of his hand refused to leave her body.

"Celebrate new baby?" The drycleaner pointed to Kimberley's middle. "You still skinny, but nothing get past me."

She smiled, nodding. "Yes, I'm pregnant."
"You give away with rub. All pregnant lady rub tummy."

* * *

Nearly thirty minutes past reservation time, waiting at the restaurant's bar, Kimberley stared at this evening's competition. *Ladies and gentlemen, Kimberley Roderick is no match for this fine amber liquid aged to perfection over eighteen years, served neat, with a water back.*

"It's just one, Kimmy."

"I know." But he'd wagered four hundred on Tiger Woods in the Masters, and after the first eighteen holes, Tiger led by four strokes. A good day on the gambling circuit meant in the hands of her husband, one whiskey would multiply. Like Gremlins. Like hamsters. Like the number of shivers up her spine whenever Luke stood within a thirty-foot radius.

"When do you think we should tell Allie?"

"About what?" She blinked away ponderings of Luke's naked, sinewy body slowly screwing into his faceless wife—God, what a lucky woman—and focused on her husband.

"About the baby."

"Not for a while."

His determined frown wrinkled his brow, and the glass again met his lips. "I was hoping to tell my parents tomorrow, and they won't be able to keep it a secret."

"Well, maybe they'll have to."

He fondled the glass as if it were the first breast he'd ever seen, in calming strokes, reassuring himself he was, in fact, touching it. "Nothing pleases you. Mom and Dad are going to love this news, and you want to keep it to yourself. Forget that you told Rick and Lauren. Forget that they told everyone else. Let my parents hear about it through the grapevine. Word travels fast in this circle of friends."

"I've been up since daybreak, and I haven't eaten in eight hours. Do you honestly think I have the energy to field this tirade?" She pressed her fingers against her forehead. "I have a pounding headache."

"What a surprise." Brennan gulped his demonic liquid. "I wish I knew what to do to make you smile. You have a new car, a custom home, a great little girl, time to spend with her, and you're healthily pregnant for the second—make that the third—time. Will you ever be happy?"

"I'm just tired, Brennan."

"You're tired all the time."

"Well, I'm pregnant. Why don't you try it sometime?" Tears welled in her eyes. *Hormones.* "Why don't you try single-handedly incubating another human being? Of course I'm tired, Brennan. I wake up tired."

"My grandmother heard that, and she's been dead for a decade." He gulped again, finishing the whiskey, and placed the glass on the lower rim of the bar's surface across from him. Great. He wanted another.

Suddenly one drink turned into two. And Kimberley had the distinct pleasure of watching him annihilate himself. "I don't necessarily think we should keep it a secret. But if we tell Allie, she'll ask every day for the next eight months if the baby's coming home yet." She dropped a hand onto Brennan's in a gentle caress, attempting to win at least one round in this fight. "Eight months is a long time for her to wait, Bren. That's all I meant."

"I guess so."

"Mr. Roderick." The young, pretty hostess mispronounced their last name and tapped Brennan on the shoulder with two fingers. "I apologize for the delay. Your table is ready."

Brennan helped Kimberley off the barstool, and they followed the sex kitten to a remote table.

"The manager would like to offer a round of complimentary drinks to make up for your wait."

"Well, that certainly isn't necessary." Brennan smiled.

And Round One goes to Kimb—

Brennan palmed a bill, handing it to the hostess. "But I appreciate the sentiment. Two Jacks. Neat."

Round One goes to the enemy. Nice try, Kimberley.

* * *

"I'll drive," she said, stepping off the curb at the valet station.

"I'm fine."

"Far from it."

With a guttural groan, he curled his lip. "Very well, James. The Depot for a little healthy competition at the dart board and a round of drinks. On me, of course."

She took a deep breath and slid behind the wheel.

"How 'bout it, Kimmy Coco Bop? We can catch the end of the Cubs game."

"I don't think so, Bren. I'm too tired."

"Well, how 'bout you take me, drop me off, and I'll take a cab home?"

"I'd like you to come home with me." Not really, but she'd take the lesser of two evil drunks.

"Okay." He sighed like a little boy dragging his toe in the sand. "I'll go home with you."

Jason entered her mind, answering her prayer for comfort. She imagined her arms around him, their naked bodies entwined in blissful slumber. The idyllic dream carried her along the way home, muffling her husband's half-asleep babblings about not having any fun now that he was married.

"The Depot." Brennan snapped his eyes open and straightened in his seat. "Kimmy, you missed the turn."

"I thought you were coming home."

"I'll be home in an hour. We've seen each other a lot today. I'll have one fast drink, and then, I promise, I'll be home to do naughty things to you."

Gee, she couldn't wait. But she'd become good at faking it. "That'll be nice."

* * *

At four in the morning, half asleep and with an achingly full bladder, Kimberley reached instinctively with her right arm and stroked Brennan's empty pillow. *Oh, God, what's he up to now?*

She peeled herself out of bed and pattered to the spacious master bath, relieved the pressure, and commenced searching the house for her passed-out husband.

No signs of him. No dirt trekked across the floor, no snacks spilled in the kitchen, no television on. He wasn't home.

With an overflowing French custard dish—blue crystal, a wedding gift from Lauren—of raspberry sherbet, she headed back to their bedroom. Eating in the middle of the night during pregnancy was a great way to monumentally expand her waistline. She shrugged. It was good to be good—really good—at something, and since she'd abandoned her career to raise children, weight gain would have to be her forte.

Was Jason a father yet? The youngest of five, he'd wanted a large family. Did he ever think about the one they'd opted against? Probably not. That sort of history haunted and followed women, but men tended to forget about it quickly. Men didn't end pregnancies—women did.

* * *

Over the years, Luke's leaving the bedroom, if not the house, at random hours of the night had become a usual practice. Caleb and Rachael slept soundly through the noises he made in departure—face-washing, teeth-brushing, even the opening of the garage door hadn't stirred them. As far as he knew, his kids were oblivious to the fact that, while he returned before sunrise, he left his wife four or five times a week.

Derby grumbled, not quite asleep on the back doormat, as if protesting Luke's early morning trek.

"Are you coming or not?" he whispered and buttoned a flannel jacket.

A slow blink answered him.

"Let's just see where she lives. Innocent, harmless, and I promise, we won't even get out of the car."

His ears perked with the sound of a favorite word.

"That's right, Derby. Car. Let's go."

With some difficulty, the canine slumped to his feet and sauntered toward the garage.

"Just for a look." Because he couldn't possibly have the piece of Kimberley he really wanted, a peek at her home would have to suffice.

Outside a gated community about twenty minutes from home, he held his breath in prayer, punching in an old passcode. It had been weeks since he'd done trim work in the neighborhood, but the service entrance gate creaked open.

Hallelujah!

Although the lantern-lit Hidden Creek Lane was deserted in the dead of night, the humungous houses looked serene, as if the well-kept landscape protected them from outside forces. Like him.

He stopped in front of number thirty-two, the only house with a front porch light on. A replica of an English country cottage, complete with oozing mortar and round turret, a light shone through a window on the second story of the tower. And through the sheers, he saw Kimberley's silhouette. All that wild, curly hair, thin arms, more-than-a-handful breasts... Elation rushed through him. "She's beautiful, isn't she, boy?"

She sat, hugging a knee and licking a spoon. *Atta girl. Eat.*

Seconds later, she swept aside the curtains and peered out the window, as if sensing his presence. He eased his foot off the brake and rolled on. God, it felt good to see her, to know she was safe.

Halfway home, a realization stirred like spoiled meat in the pit of his stomach. She was alone. And waiting. More than likely for her absent husband. And Luke's being there had probably given her false hope.

An urge swelled in his heart to turn around, bundle her in his arms, and rescue her and her daughter from that posh hotel of loneliness. But no matter how strong the pull, her situation wasn't his business. Not yet anyway.

And he had problems of his own to face, torn between his growing feelings for a woman he barely knew and the shadow of love for his wife.

When he climbed back into bed, he touched Diane's cheek, careful not to wake her, wondering if he ever left her feeling as alone as Kimberley looked in that turret.

Probably. But military duty in Saudi Arabia was hardly a vacation.

CHAPTER 5

Creeeeeeak!

Awakened by the disturbing sound, he focused on the clock. Six-oh-six in the morning.

The television clicked on, and he rolled over to see his wife stationed before a full-sized ironing board in their bedroom, a basket of linens on the floor next to her, and her favorite soap opera, taped from yesterday afternoon, displayed on the screen.

He sighed. "Good morning."

"Did I wake you? Sorry about that, but I've been asking you for months to oil the hinge on my ironing board."

He crawled out of bed and headed toward the one luxury their home boasted: an attached master bathroom. "Do you have to iron right now? And right here?"

"Well, your damn dog woke me before five to go out, but I suppose you didn't hear that."

"Sorry."

"And he didn't make it in time. Dribbled all the way down the stairs."

"I'll clean it up." He shoved his toothbrush into his mouth.

"You think I'd let it sit there? I already took care of it. That's the second time this past week."

"He's getting old," he said through a mouthful of toothpaste. "He's losing control. It's not his fault."

"Put him down, Luke. This is no way to live."

"Are you talking about Derby's quality of life, or your own?"

"I don't have time to worry about quality when the quantity of laundry in this house surpasses that of a third-world orphanage. You wear more clothes than—"

"Kick me next time." He spat into the sink. "And I'll get up."

"Just like you'll oil the hinge on the ironing board," she muttered. "Useless."

I hate her. He didn't recognize the angry man in the mirror staring back at him, but before he even cleaned the toothpaste from his chin, he bounded toward the stairs, raced through the kitchen, and headed into the basement, to his small workshop. He wiped the toothpaste off with his bare forearm, opened a homemade cabinet, and pulled a small can of WD40 from a shelf.

All right, she *did* ask him to oil the hinge, but on the same day his sister had miscarried, the same day of Caleb's winter concert at school, and the same day Rachael lost her first tooth. He did all he could that day.

He'd invoiced twelve hundred dollars, encouraged Julie to try again, went to three banks to find three crisp two-dollar bills for the Tooth Fairy, and sat in the front row to see his son's rendition of *Frosty the Snowman*. And he'd oil the damn hinge right now.

When he returned to the bedroom, Diane, engrossed in Haley's love affair with Stone, was ironing a king-sized sheet.

"Excuse me." He tossed the sheet to the floor.

She backed away, and, judging by the hatred in her eyes, she wanted to press the hot iron to his crotch. "You can't do this at a convenient time?"

"Can't you?" He ducked under the board and aimed at the hinge. "Why are you ironing sheets anyway? We're just going to sleep in them."

"They're one hundred percent cotton, Luke."

"So?" He popped up and tested the hinge. Creak-free and smooth.

"So, they come out of the dryer wrinkled."

"They've got to wrinkle somehow." He yanked the sheet up from the floor and threw it back onto the board. "It's not like we're rolling around in them or anything."

"Are you going to counseling this week?"

"Yeah."

"Why don't you ask Dr. Schaeffer why you're obsessed with sticking your dick into holes?"

"Why don't you come with me and ask him why the bolt at your knees needs more oiling than that hinge?"

She shot him with an icy stare. Whoever said eyes were the windows to someone's soul had never looked into Diane's. Iced-over blue, they hadn't warmed in nearly eight years. "Don't you have work to do? Somewhere to be, other than here?"

"What?" Every muscle in his body unclenched.

"Just…go. Somewhere. Anywhere."

"You want me to go." If he couldn't win her with kindness, anger sure as hell wouldn't do the trick. He exhaled a calm, controlled breath. "Do you ever miss me, Diane?"

"How can I miss you? You're here, underfoot, all the time. Christ, even when you leave me, you're on my phone every two hours."

"Do you miss us, I mean? What we used to be?"

"No." Her lips formed a hard line. "Not anymore."

"I'm not asking for much."

"Neither am I. I just want you to leave me alone."

* * *

"Where's Daddy?" Allison asked.

Kimberley, dreading the question all morning, tucked a curl behind her daughter's ear. "Where do you think he is?"

Allison petted Kimberley's diamond and spun the ring around her mother's finger, a threadbare, pink rabbit dangling from her other hand. "Working?"

"Maybe he is." An online look at their checking account showed a two-hundred-dollar debit at two a.m. Brennan had never been gone this long before, and her heart trembled with horrifying thoughts. Maybe he was bleeding on a highway median, fucking a stripper, or running from some irate giant to whom he'd lost a ridiculous bet. Worst of all, chances were he'd yet to pull himself out of the drunken stupor she'd left him in at the Depot last night.

"Could we call him, Mommy?"

She'd called him no less than twenty-seven times, to no avail. "I have a better idea. Let's call Auntie Lauren for a play date."

Allison's violet-blue eyes sparkled like forget-me-nots in the rain. "A play date today? Can Pink come?"

"Yes. You and Pink can play with Deacon and the girls, and maybe I'll pick up Daddy. How does that sound?"

Allison screeched a giggle, prompting Kimberley to dial her best friend. "Lauren, I need a favor."

"Absolutely."

"I need you to watch Allison."

"That's not a favor, Kim. It's a pleasure. When?"

"Well...now, and unfortunately, I don't know when I'll be picking her up. I have to go looking for Brennan, and—"

"What do you mean, go looking for Brennan?"

"I mean I can't find him. I don't know where he is."

"Honey."

"He didn't come home last night."

"He's fine, honey, he's fine. Probably just now waking up. Screw him, he'll find his way home."

"Still, I'd feel better—"

"Of course I'll take Allie, and you go shopping. Buy something for yourself. And I'm not talking napkin rings, I'm talking armoire. Maybe a new settee for your breakfast room."

"I like the one I have."

"Hit back where it hurts. Call that professor at UIC, leave a voicemail, tell him you're fiercely interested in that position, and wait for the calls to roll in."

"I don't know." The professor wouldn't likely care if she called, but she knew what *would* redeem her squashed esteem. And this time, she'd go straight to the jogging path at the preserve to find him.

*   *   *

Thirty minutes later, she lounged on a blanket, about to surrender to much-needed sleep. He wasn't going to show. Dumb idea, waiting for him. Doubly hurt, she began to gather the things she'd brought with her. He was probably at home, naked and entwined with his wife. Stupid to think he might keep his usual routine for the sole chance she'd be waiting for him someday. Sure, he'd held her hand, but that didn't mean—

"Hey, Kimber."

She blinked up, her heart racing, to see him jogging in place. "Hi, Luke. How are you?"

"What are you doing here?"

"Thinking."

"About what?"

"Why don't you have a seat?"

His nose wrinkled, as if it itched, and he jogged his way over. "I'm kind of dirty and sweaty, but—"

"I don't mind."

He plopped down next to her, a single bead of sweat dripping at his temple. "How long have we known each another?"

Seven days, twenty-one hours, and forty-three minutes. "I don't know. A week, maybe."

"So, are you ever going to answer me outright, or do I have to butter your bread every time? Let's try this again." He wiped his brow and boldly tucked his sweaty hand against her stomach. "Are you looking for me?"

"I'm just here. Thinking."

"About what?" His fingers tapped against her.

"Sex."

"Sex." His lips parted into a delicious grin.

"About having it. With a man who loves me."

"This man have a name, Kimberley, or are you inventing him out of thin air?" He licked his upper lip.

"That all depends on whether I'm remembering him in his true capacity or building him up in my mind."

He squinted into a beam of sunlight and tickled her stomach. "I love the taste of pregnant women." His back met the ground, but his hand maintained its intimate contact.

Heat crept into her cheeks. To think of Luke's perfect mouth pressed against her vagina—

"Do you have a deep, soft cunt? I mean, most mothers do, but I'll bet you know how to use yours."

"I beg your pardon?" She hadn't meant to whisper.

He shrugged, massaging her stomach. "There's something about childbirth that creates a deep, soft pocket in the birth canal. Did that happen to you?"

"How would I know?"

"What? You've never felt it? Feel it now. Go ahead. I won't look."

I'd rather you watched. "Absolutely not."

"Just do it, Kimber." His voice, tender and dreamy, lulled her. A bedroom voice, if she'd ever heard one. "Slide that dainty hand down your pants and stick a finger in. Up to your wedding ring."

"Do you request this sort of thing often?"

"If I did, *I'd* be inside you." His hand slithered down to her lap and grazed, for a split second, against the clothing that covered her most private parts.

When did she part her legs?

"What would your wife say about this conversation?"

"One less thing she has to do with me, not that she does it with me anyway." He closed his eyes and drummed his hands against his stomach. "But I don't get it anywhere else, except in the shower, with myself."

What an image—this hunk of a man gratifying himself, dripping wet. His hand jerking over his cock, the muscles in his back tensing. Water trailing in rivulets off his shoulders. A crease forming in his brow with his strokes becoming more determined, about to—

Oh, my. Such a waste. She owed it to women everywhere to straddle him. Could she drink Luke the way Brennan drank whiskey? Could she wager her family-shmamily the way her husband tossed out Ben Franklins for random RBIs?

She locked her gaze on Luke's closed eyes, tucked a finger under her shorts, and pressed it into her vagina. Moist and tight, and it felt good. Ready.

Luke parted his lips and sighed, as if he'd felt the pleasure along with her.

She dragged her finger out and buried it again.

"Do you like sex?" he asked.

"Yes." She added another finger to the mix, filling her void more thoroughly. Her juices accumulated under her fingernails, and she prodded, but it still wasn't enough. Did she have a deep cunt? She needed Luke inside her, to fill and satisfy her, to judge for himself.

"It feels good?"

"Yes."

"Diane says it hasn't felt good for her since my boy was born."

With the mention of his wife, she snapped her fingers out, suddenly feeling silly. "Did it..." She cleared her throat and wiped her wet fingers against the blanket. "Did it feel good before he was born?"

"I thought so, but what do I know?"

"Maybe she holds you responsible. Maybe she thinks she missed out on a lot because of the way things happened."

"Because I got her pregnant before we were married?"

"Maybe."

He shook his head. "So tell me what you feel like."

"No."

"I wasn't watching."

Her breath caught in her throat.

"Did you do it?" He peeled his eyes open. "Did you feel yourself?"
She gave a quick nod. "Yes."
"Because I asked? Or because you wanted to?"
"Truth first. You don't cheat on your wife?"
"Answer my question," he whispered with a smile.
"Both. Now you answer mine. Do you cheat?"
"I don't, but I have." His hand wandered back onto her stomach. "In the Army, in Saudi."
"Were you married at the time?"
"No."
"Planning on it?"
"Not formally."
"So you cheated, but you didn't commit adultery. There's a difference."
"Yeah, but there's one other time I'm not particularly proud of. When she was pregnant with Caleb, we hadn't had sex in months, and I got a blowjob at a bachelor party."
"Did you pay for it? Or was it from the bachelor?"
"No." He smiled. "And no. You're funny, though."
The heat of his hand moving on her belly rushed like wildfire, sending surges to her nipples, which hardened with the anticipation of his touch.
"We were up in Lake Geneva. I ran into this girl I used to know, and she was wearing blood-red lipstick. Vampire red, you know? Trashy, but classy at the same time. I told her I'd like to see what it looked like smeared on my boxer shorts. Evidently, so did she."
"That's it? You commented on her lipstick, and she dropped to her knees?"
"Right there under the table in a crowded bar."
"Some girl."
"Nothing next to you."
"You don't know me."
"You're just so pretty. You're pretty enough I don't have to know you to know how amazing you are. And you don't have to know me. I've never met someone that I just…clicked with before."
She searched his eyes for a gleam of mischief, but only honesty poured out at her.
"My kids mean everything to me," he said.
"Mine, too."
"But I wish I'd had them with someone else. I can't leave Diane.

Six months without my children was hell, and I know I can't do that again."

"We can get custody of your children." For half a second, she imagined escaping with him, their four collective babies in tow.

"We?"

Her cheeks grew hot. "I guess that sounded rather suggestive—"

"Thrilling."

"Before Allie was born, I was a lawyer. Family law."

"Oh. For a second there, I thought..." Their gazes met. "I thought you were going to tell me to run away with you."

She took a deep breath and began to shake her head, refusing to admit just how close she'd come. "I helped pay for our house. Brennan forgets that once I had a career."

"You still have one, Kimberley."

"Not much challenge in wiping her nose."

"You don't like being home?"

"No, I do. It's just, you know, all I went through, searching for a way to make it happen—grants, scholarships, all the essays and interviews—and for what?"

"Listen. It's easy for a stay-at-home mother to feel worthless, but it's the most important—and the most difficult—job on earth. I see what Diane goes through day-to-day, and I tell you, I don't know many men who could do it. You're unbelievable. Don't forget that."

"What's unbelievable is I aborted Jason's child so I could go to law school, and now I'm a housewife."

"You had an abortion?"

Oh, wow. She'd told him her darkest secret. "I don't want to talk about it."

"All right."

A man in emerald green sweats jogged past, but Luke refused to take his eyes off her. He wove a hand into hers.

"So do you think you'll ever go back to being a lawyer?"

"No, but I might teach at UIC. Political science, history. Brennan doesn't want me to, but—"

"Teachers are good people." His mesmerizing pink tongue slipped across his lips. "And you'll be a good teacher."

She took a deep breath, staring at his tempting mouth. Why did she feel as if she could tell him anything, and he'd accept her no matter what? "Jason left it up to me."

Luke squeezed her hand.

"I don't think it's what he wanted, but he let me make the decision." He pressed their entwined hands to her gestating baby. "I wish it were mine."

"Why do you say things like that? You don't know anything about me."

"I know you're still in love with a man who left you. I know I remind you of him. And the one thing I know for certain is the way that makes me feel."

She wriggled away from his touch. "How dare you assume you know my feelings?"

"How dare you assume I don't?" He grinned.

"And what makes you believe you're worthy enough to join Jason's rank?"

"Anyone's worthy, Kimberley. He left you, so he's not worth the quarter to call him, and you still love him. I can't figure it out."

She wanted to slap him.

She wanted to tear his head off.

She wanted to have his children.

"I don't even know what you're talking about," she said. "I'm obviously not in love with—"

"Relax. You're human, and you're entitled to human feelings. It doesn't mean you have to act on them."

She rubbed away a tear. When had she started crying? *Damn hormones.* "I don't know how I feel, but I know I married a man who doesn't love me."

"My God, Kimberley, look at you. You married a man who doesn't deserve you. Period."

"You don't know my husband either. He gives me everything he can."

"That might be true, but he doesn't give you what he should."

"You married a woman who won't sleep with you."

"I know." He brushed his right hand against her cheek and caught a tear. "I know my situation is just as ridiculous as yours."

"If you aren't happy, Luke, leave your wife. But I won't sit here while you try to convince me your happiness hinges upon mine." She stood, drawing in a long, shuddered breath, and wiping the last tears from her cheeks. "It's absurd really."

"But everything's about you. I told you before—I don't do this kind of thing."

"You're not fooling me. And women don't randomly suck dick

under bar tables."

"Did you just say...I mean, actually say..." He shook his head. "Wow. Look, Kimberley. I wish I understood why I've been thinking of you since I saw you. I wish I could stop thinking about you because it isn't fair to my children."

"I agree."

"But since I caught you when you were falling, I can't stop thinking about how soft you are, how pretty your little mouth is. And I can't stop wishing you'd fall for me someday."

"Stop," she said, much more quietly than she'd intended.

"I told you before. I'm married, I'm harmless, and I don't cheat on my wife."

"Then stop trying to. Give me an inch of respect, will you?" She began to back away.

"I'll give you seven-and-five-eighths."

"You've measured it." With a roll of her eyes, she turned away.

A deep chuckle resonated behind her. "Come on, Kimber. That was a joke."

"I have to get home," she said over her shoulder. "And wait for my husband."

"I'll be thinking of you," he called after her.

* * *

He watched until she was out of sight, his fingers caressing the satin edge of the blanket she'd left behind. *What a woman.* Talk about being ready to burst through his pants! She'd actually fingered herself on his request.

He balled the blanket, tucked it under his arm, and walked the rest of the jogging path in quiet serenity. This woman had come into his life for a reason, and by God, he'd be there whenever she was ready.

Derby grumbled when Luke slid onto the truck's bench seat. "What, boy? Can you smell her on me? Take a good whiff." The old dog sniffed his master's hand, his soft tongue taking a lap against his palm. "All right, all right. Let's go home."

Upon reaching the white tri-level with the impeccably mowed lawn, Luke helped the dog from the cab and entered through the garage door.

"What's that?" Diane stood at the washing machine, nodding at the light green mass in his hands.

Oh, hell. Kimberley's blanket.

* * *

Kimberley hesitated before entering the house, an empty space in her stomach. What would she do if Brennan hadn't returned, if she found a message from the police department on the voice mail, requesting she identify her husband's drunken, dead body?

Her hands trembled as she turned the knob, but a familiar warmth welcomed her into the mudroom, a calming reassurance of cherry wood lockers—Brennan's was empty, but he never put anything in it—and floral potpourri. *Home.*

She brushed at a smudge of dirt on her white T-shirt, where Luke had rested his hand. Suddenly, his scent accosted her. Wintergreen chewing gum. Fabric softener. Musky-male-out-running. He'd barely touched her, but he was all over her.

Could others smell him on her, too? She should shower the scent of him away. Now. "Brennan?"

No answer.

With a pounding, nervous heart, she climbed the stairs and entered the master sitting room, immediately removing her T-shirt. And with it, the sexual scent of Luke.

"Kimmy, I'm sorry."

She dropped her T-shirt and spun toward her husband's voice. He sat on the sofa, with the Masters coverage blaring on the television. His red, puffy eyes suggested he'd been crying, but she knew better. He'd spent the morning up-chucking, wherever he'd slept.

She raised a hand, continuing toward the shower. "I don't want to hear it."

"Kimmy, I love you."

"Show me, you son-of-a-bitch. Prove it to me."

"I don't know what happened last night. I'm sorry."

"I don't care how sorry you claim to be." *Luke* was all over her, like Chanel No. 5. The only thing she cared about was hitting that shower before Brennan came close enough to pick up the scent.

"Where's Allie?"

"What do you care?" She ripped *Luke* from her body and shed the rest of her clothing.

"What do I care? She's my daughter, too, you know."

"Yes, I know. I know it all too well. That doesn't mean you deserve her." Did Luke's abstinent wife ever feel this same abandonment? Did Diane feel alone when her husband spent the morning jogging, or placing his hands on other women's bodies? Allowing his life to carry on, despite his fatherly obligation?

Did Luke's seven-and-five-eighths crave her favorite shade of lipstick the way she yearned for an hour of Brennan's undivided attention?

"Kimmy?" Brennan appeared in the bathroom doorway, while she sobbed against the glass shower doors, steaming water beating onto her head.

"She's with Lauren and Rick. If your blood-alcohol content is legal, go get her."

"I'm sorry." He unbuttoned the collar on his golf shirt.

"You aren't sorry, and you don't love me. And don't even think about joining me now."

"Too late." He dropped his pants. "Already thought about it, already decided to."

"Have a conventional affair, will you? With a live, breathing woman. Stop putting up hundreds for a few dozen drinks and a high score, and start spending it on a legitimate, trashy blonde. Leave me for her, for all I care, but I can't do this anymore."

"You don't want that." He entered the shower.

She turned her back to him. "Yes, that's exactly what I want. Not one soul recognizes your problem as an infidelity, but it hurts worse than cheating ever could."

His hand slithered around to her abdomen.

Luke. Nerves swirled into desire. Oh, to feel that man's wet body behind hers, to save him from chronic self-pleasure with a grip around his thick seven-and-five-eighths.

"How's our baby?"

She parted her legs for Luke, imagining his strong hand entering her one finger at a time until he plunged her with all four, hitting every inch and massaging her clitoris with his thumb.

"I'd be crazy not to love you," he whispered, kissing the hollow of her collarbone. "You're beautiful."

When a hand wandered over her breasts, she shook in his embrace, biological urges overtaking her. In her mind, it wasn't her husband pumping inside of her, bringing her to orgasm.

It was Luke, stroking her just right, whispering words of encouragement, building her up. Her breasts tingling, her clit surging with power, with pleasure.

"Oh, my God." Her orgasm broke in an intense rush, and she caught her breath.

"That's my girl," Brennan whispered, with a slap to her ass.

She blinked away water and pushed away from her husband.

"Not done with you yet," he said.

"Well, I'm done with you." She'd used him the way he'd used the old No. 7 last night—for a brief thrill, far from reciprocal.

"What?" He brushed water from his face and, standing ramrod erect, attempted to close the door before she strode through it. He was unsuccessful.

"I'm done." She dressed and left to retrieve her daughter.

CHAPTER 6

"We have the room, Luke." Julie Sheffield placed a plate of leftover chicken casserole onto the kitchen table in front of her big brother. "Move back in."

"I appreciate the offer." Derby slept on his feet under the table, numbing his legs. "But it isn't that easy," he said between mouthfuls of comfort food, Julie's specialty.

"I don't like to see you this way. When was the last time you slept?"

Sleeping with an erection was nearly impossible, but more than that, his mind wandered at night. If he married Kimberley someday, would she hate him in five years the way Diane did now? Would she roll away in the middle of the night to avoid his touch? "I think we might be happy."

"You and Diane? Are you serious?"

He looked up. "You know I try with Diane, right? I mean, you know I give it my all, right?"

"You give it more than you should."

"Well, I'm done. I'm done giving."

"It's about damn time."

"I'm not leaving her. I'm just done. I met someone."

"Oh, Luke." Her knitted brow displayed her disappointment, the same way it did when she was a child. "Are you having an affair?"

"Not yet."

"This isn't what you need."

"Easy for you to say. You're secure with a great house, an attentive husband, and you'll have everything you've ever wanted once this baby's born."

"We're not talking about me, and it's easy for anyone to say. What's so difficult to understand? You're married, albeit to the devil, and until you divorce her, what do you see happening between you and this woman? Sex? Because if sex is all you're after—"

"No." He shoveled the last of the casserole into his mouth. "We're good together."

"Is she married?"

"And pregnant."

"I can't believe I'm hearing this." Julie shook her head, her rich, brown hair bouncing against her shoulders. "If you're not happy, Luke, leave your wife."

"Why does every woman I know suggest that?"

"I don't know…because it's the sane thing to do, maybe? What does Dr. Schaeffer say?"

"I can't leave her without leaving my kids, and I promised Caleb a long time ago—" A crack of thunder drowned his words, but the promise he'd made to his son was no secret to his sister.

"You told Caleb you wouldn't leave again." She stood and reached for his empty plate. "Luke, he's eight. Are you going to hang around for another ten years, living like this, in order to keep some ridiculous promise you never should have made?"

"Thirteen years, at least, until Rachael's in college."

"You're going to screw around for thirteen years?"

"I don't think Diane would notice. I walked into the house the other day with a blanket—this woman's blanket we shared at the forest preserve—and you know what? She washed it without blinking an eye."

"Finish with one woman before you start with another. You know how I feel about your wife, but she did have two children for you, and she probably deserves the courtesy. There's nothing more humiliating than a cheating spouse." She walked to the sink, where she rinsed the dish, unaware Luke knew exactly how humiliating a cheating spouse could be, but…

"How do you know what a cheating spouse is like?"

She shook her head. "Don't worry about it."

"Julie? Is there something about Bobby you're not telling me?"

"No, but that's another thing. If this woman is willing to cheat on one husband, why wouldn't she cheat on another?"

"There are circumstances. And who says she's willing? She needs some convincing."

She stared hard at him, just starting to show, never looking as healthy. "Do you really want to get involved with this woman's circumstances?"

"Half of me says no."

"Then the other half of you better wake the hell up."

"This isn't black and white, Julie. Do you think I want things this way?"

"Do you still love Diane?"

Unable to voice the obvious answer, he shrugged. "Can anyone love a woman like that?"

"Get a good lawyer."

He pulled his feet out from under the dog and stamped them against the floor to stimulate circulation. Kimberley was a lawyer, and he'd bet she was good in every capacity.

"Our door is always open. We're a five-minute drive away. It's not like you'd be leaving the way Dad did."

* * *

"I want to call Daddy." Allison cuddled against Kimberley under piles of blankets, sweating and shivering at the same time. Her temperature had risen to a hundred-and-two, and she'd thrown up twice in the past hour.

And to make matters worse, morning sickness churned through Kimberley's gut, like a wave slowly approaching a rocky shore. When would it hit? And with a hot bulk of child lying across her, would she make it to the toilet when it did? "Shh. Daddy'll be home soon."

"When?"

She glanced at the clock. Six minutes until seven. After a few days out of state, Brennan finished his week at the Elgin Riverboat Casino, entertaining new recruits with a late luncheon, drinks, and—of course—card games galore. His ETA was anyone's guess.

"Mommy? Are you sick, too?"

"Yes, Allie."

"Let's call Daddy. He'll come."

"All right, let's try him again." She reached for the cordless phone on the nightstand and dialed.

"Yeah?" Brennan answered after several rings.

"It's me."

"Hi, Kimmy. How's our little girl?"

Although he labored to sound sober, Kimberley guessed by the inflection in his voice that he was far from it. "Not well."

"Want me to come home?"

"It'd be nice."

Only the background noise of a casino bar sounded over the line until Brennan cleared his throat. "You can't handle this?"

"Brennan, I'm exhausted. It's been a long week."

"You know that's how I feel all the time, right?"

You have the energy to stay out playing games until four in the morning. "Brennan, please."

He sighed like a teenager whose parents had denied him the car keys. "This outing is the best part of my job. I've got one-fifty on Gretchen."

"Who?"

"It's a reality show. Sixteen strangers deserted on Route 66, and the last one to the check point is out of the race. I bet on Gretchen."

"You're kidding, right? Allie is sick, and she hasn't stopped asking for you."

"Let me enjoy this."

"Brennan, I think this is a special circumstance. I'm not feeling well either."

"I forgot. You're the only woman in the world who's ever had a baby."

Spoken like a true man. She hung up.

"I wanted to talk." Allison sniffled. "I miss Daddy."

"Shh. He's coming, baby. It's all right. He's coming." If she'd married Jason, he would have been halfway home by now, on a rescue mission.

It hit her for the first time. Jason *had* tried to rescue her on the eve of her wedding day. With the letter on which she still depended. Perhaps he wrote it by design, knowing she would keep it. Knowing she'd need a piece of him for the rest of her life.

Allison eventually cried herself to sleep, and Kimberley slipped from the bed. She washed her face and brushed her teeth before sauntering toward the kitchen. She retrieved *The Fabulous Gourmet*, and it fell open to the hollandaise page. Perhaps it was time to move Jason's letter to the dessert section, lest her husband find it. Or maybe she ought to toss it. After all those years, keeping it was probably unhealthy.

She crumbled the sheet of paper—she'd done so countless times to date—and tossed it into the already full wastebasket. There. Jason was gone, and now she could concentrate on her life. The life she'd chosen to live.

She tapped her toes against the floor and darted glances at the waste basket. *I'm okay with my decision. Really, I don't need that letter.*

After a few more glances, she jumped to retrieve the wad, ironed it with her hands, and tucked it back into the hollandaise page. Some things were never meant to leave her.

The telephone rang and she pounced on it. She didn't have the energy to rock Allison back to sleep, so she didn't waste time checking the caller ID.

"Hey, Kimberley." A vaguely familiar, male voice.

She scanned the window on the back of the receiver. She didn't recognize the number.

"It's Luke, beautiful girl."

Her stomach flip-flopped. How did he find her unlisted number? And why the hell was he using it?

"Kimberley?"

"What do you want?"

"You're hard to find. Would you believe it took a twenty at the club counter to get your number?"

Talkative towel boys.

"Kimberley, are you there?"

"Yeah. What do you want?"

"This is a pretty bad storm, and I know your husband's never around to take care of you, so—"

"Is it raining?" She peeked out from behind a shade for the first time since morning. Rain poured in sheets. "Well, at least Allison and I didn't miss a sunny day."

"Go back to the window."

"How did you—"

"I want to see what you're wearing."

Her heart quickened and she snapped up the shade. And there before her, with a tiny cell phone pressed to his ear, stood Luke, holding a magazine above his head to shelter his perfect hair from the rain, illuminated with the outside lights. Her jaw slowly dropped.

"I was in the neighborhood. I'm not stalking you or anything like that."

Pity.

"I just..." He shrugged. "I don't know, I wanted to see you."

"Now you have."

"Nice nightgown."

A white cotton, chemise style, there was nothing sexy about it.

"It's very"—he paused, cocking his head, studying her through dripping panes of glass—"maternal."

"Go home."

"Where's your daughter?"

"She's asleep. You shouldn't be here."

"Is your husband home?"

"No."

"Then give me two minutes." He smiled.

"No. Go home." Desire twitched between her legs; perhaps it was time to use the purple vibrator Brennan hid in her Christmas stocking last year.

She stared at the delicious man in her driveway. Because he was already soaking wet, it was easy to imagine Luke's self-gratification in the shower. *Oh, what an image.*

"Ninety seconds," he said.

"Forty-five, starting three seconds ago."

He hitched his chin toward the back door. "Let me in."

"Absolutely not."

"Then come outside."

"It's raining."

"Don't you have to take the garbage out or something?"

She glanced at the overflowing can. "Yes, actually. How did you know that?"

"Women let it pile up and that's all right. It isn't ladies' work."

"Good-bye, Luke." She hung up and pulled the shade down. The sound of the rain lulled her, now that she was aware of it. Her nausea had subsided, but the image of Luke in the rain left her far from content.

A nagging sensation drew her toward the trash bin. Because she was insane—*I must be*—she gathered the plastic bag, secured it with a twist tie, and yanked it out of the can.

While she could have reached the attached garage through the mudroom, she exited into the screened porch and out onto the open-air patio. Warm rain bled through her nightgown, stimulating her nipples.

He stood less than three feet away, but she carried on as if he were a mirage, tossed the bag into the city-issued receptacle, and pivoted back toward the house. A small stick wedged between her toes, and she bent at the waist to remove it.

Even through the downpour, she heard Luke's heavy sigh. He'd probably caught sight of her thong panties. She continued onward in the rain, pretending not to see him, and disappeared into the breakfast room.

By the time she'd reached the kitchen window to steal a glance in his direction, he'd gone, but the sensation in her clitoris remained.

Instantly ashamed of her actions, of the insatiable craving between her legs, she hung her head.

She loved her husband.

She adored her daughter.

She was carrying her husband's second baby...

She placed a hand around one a breast, enjoying the feel of thin, wet cotton clinging to her body. Fantasizing about gorgeous Luke hiking up her skirt against a drenched maple tree, entering her hard amid a ruthless downpour, that mysterious scar near his eye crinkling with a determined squint.

Her other hand traveled to her damp panties.

...but what she really wanted was the stranger who wanted her.

* * *

"Put away the Play Station, Caleb." Luke strummed his fingers on the painted pine molding—standard issue in homes like his—that framed the family room doorway. Diane glared from her chair across the room, where she read. Luke dodged the daggers and looked back to his son. "Bedtime."

Caleb glanced up, neglecting to follow orders. "Where'd you go, Dad?"

"Nowhere."

"Your hair's wet."

"Just an emergency call for a sump pump. Now put the games away."

Diane rustled the pages of a romance novel, noisily interfering with his parenting.

"I have one more guy left." Caleb's tongue appeared at the corner of his mouth, his trademark position for concentration.

"Caleb, I'm not going to say it again." In two steps, Luke was close enough to turn off the television.

"Dad!"

"It's way past your bedtime. Go upstairs."

"But I—"

"I'll be right up to tuck you in. Go."

Within moments, his boy stomped up the stairs, muttering about the unfairness of growing up, and Diane sneered behind this evening's reading material.

"What's so funny, Diane?"

"Nothing. Interesting that you'd lie to your son, but I wouldn't say it's funny."

"I don't lie to my children. I was over at Middlefork, checking on a sump pump for Mr. Randall." Luke shoved his hands through his damp hair. No need to tell her—or his son—about the detour down Hidden Creek Lane and the tremendous body he'd seen through wet cotton. "And what's he doing still awake? It's almost nine."

"I'm tired of being the bad guy today. Nice of you step in."

"Hey, I worked my ass off today. I do my share."

"You don't know what a share is, in this place."

"You want me to help out a little more?"

"Put your damn clothes in the hamper, take them out of the dryer and fold—"

"All right. Laundry's mine from now on."

She gave her head a shake and curled her sweatpants-clad legs under her bottom, refusing to look up from her book. "I don't want to reciprocate with blowjobs."

"Did I ask?"

"You didn't have to. I know you."

"How about a kiss?"

"I know where that'll lead."

"I guess that's all there is to say then."

"Guess so."

"The house looks nice. Thanks for straightening." He tapped a fist against the molding, keeping time with the rain, staring at his wife, waiting for her to acknowledge him.

"Do you mind?" She turned the page. "That's awfully distracting."

He'd give her "distracting." Kimberley Roderick, glowing and soaking wet. Bending over. God, it had taken everything he'd had not to pounce on her, claim her lips, and have his way with her; thus, the quick exit. And thinking about her now wasn't doing him any favors.

After one last look at his wife, he left the room and charged up the stairs. Tucked a pouting Caleb into bed. Peeked in on a sleeping Rachael. And hit the shower, more engorged than a senior on prom night.

Warm water streamed over his body, and he gripped his more-than-ready penis, stroking with gentle pressure the way he imagined Kimberley would. If he closed his eyes and ignored the sensation in his palm, it wasn't impossible to pretend the beautiful girl stood next to him.

He imagined her full, pregnant breasts tickling against his chest. Her feminine fingers working over the length of him from balls to tip. Her soft, sweet voice asking him to fill her, to love her, to let her love him.

He remembered the sight of her beautiful ass through her wet nightgown, her pretty, pink nipples peeking at him, begging for kisses. He needed to be with her again, to lay her down in satin, work her over good. Her mouth wouldn't miss an inch, swallowing the whole of his cock, and he'd blanket her with his hands, show her the reciprocity he was missing at home. He'd enter her slowly, feel her shiver.

His hand beat against his shaft without a sliver of patience, without the delicacy of a woman's touch. And, God, he missed the tenderness, but just thinking about her had to be enough. Those thighs tightening at his cheeks, the sweet drip of nectar flooding over his tongue. That's it, that's it.

* * *

At one in the morning, the telephone rang a disturbing shrill. Kimberley rolled over and reached for the receiver before Allison stirred. "Hello?"

"Love you," Brennan sang through the phone line.

"Where are you?" She climbed out of bed and headed toward the kitchen, where she could have a conversation without waking her daughter.

"Missed the last train."

"Where are you?"

"Don't know." He yawned. "Some street."

"What street?"

Only the subtle sounds of his breathing hissed through the phone line.

"Are you alone?"

No answer.

"Brennan?"

"Damn it, that's my ear."

"Look at the street signs, and tell me where you are."

"Ohio and..." Another long yawn. "Ohio and Dunston."

Ohio and Dunston. Ohio and Dunston. Ohio and Dunston. Think, Kimberley.. What's at Ohio and Dunston?

She opened her laptop and logged onto Yahoo! Maps.

"It was a bad night, Coco Bop."

"What'd you lose?"

"You don't want to know."

She keyed in *Ohio and Dunston.* "Oh. There's a Marriott just off the southwest corner. Can you see it?"

"Um..." A deep sigh resonated in her ear. "Yeah."

"Check in. Get a room, and come home tomorrow."

"If you were stuck somewhere, I'd come for you."

"Allison's asleep, Brennan, and she's sick. I can't put her in the car for a two-hour excursion at this hour. Check into the hotel."

"That's exactly what I need. Another hotel room."

"Well, what do you propose to do about your situation?"

"If you cared, you'd be here."

"Brennan."

"I don't know. I'll get a cab or something. Or I'll hitch a ride with these guys."

"Which guys?"

"I don't know, some assholes on the street. Hey!" He yelled, she assumed, to some passersby. "Where ya headed?"

"Find a taxi, but don't hitch."

"You don't give a fuck about what I'm doing." And again, speaking to someone on the street. "All I'm trying to do is get home to see her, and the bitch won't get off her ass to come get me. Tell you what. Heads, I give you fifty to take me to the North shore. Tails, we'll make it a clean one hundred."

"Bren, don't—"

"Come get me, and I won't flip the coin."

"Fine. I'm going to hang up and call you back on my cell when Allison and I are in the car."

No reply.

"Brennan?"

"Love you."

What a life. "I'll be there in an hour, all right?"

"Love you." He broke the connection.

She pulled off her nightgown, stiff from its earlier soaking, and stepped into sweats. She gathered blankets, medicine for upset stomachs, soda crackers, and a bucket—Who knew what she might need, should Allison awaken along the way?—and rushed to the garage.

With the car packed and running, she dashed back into the house to retrieve sleeping, sweating Allison and Pink the Rabbit.

"Mommy," Allison whimpered in her sleep.

Kimberley carried her to the car, carefully fastened the buckles of her car seat around her tiny body, and dialed Brennan's cell number.

"Brennan, I need you to stay on the line with me. I'm on my way, but I don't want you to fall asleep."

"I'm tired. It's been a long week."

"Don't fall asleep. Are you still at the same intersection?"

No answer.

"Brennan? Are you still at the same corner?"

"Yeah, me and the bag ladies."

"Keep talking to me, Brennan. Tell me about your day."

"Nothing special. Just work. Won one-fifty for Gretchen."

"But you lost overall?"

"I'm too tired to think about it."

"Well, so am I, but we have to keep each other awake."

"I want to tie you up tonight." He snickered.

"Good." She shuddered with the thought of it. "Tell me what else you want to do me."

"I want to videotape you."

"What else, Brennan?"

"I'm tired."

"Don't go to sleep."

No answer.

"Brennan?"

No answer.

"Brennan!"

No answer.

Within seconds, the connection broke.

"Mommy."

Kimberley reached into the backseat and comforted her daughter. "Shh, Allie, it's all right."

On the way to Elgin, constantly hitting redial, without reaching her husband, Kimberley assumed the worst. Being drunk, alone, and half-asleep, he was an easy target for a mugging. He was probably unconscious somewhere. Bleeding and as broken as her heart.

When she arrived at Ohio and Dunston, nearly an hour later, Brennan was nowhere to be seen. Drained, she bawled in defeat. "I can't do this anymore," she whispered into her hands. "I'm done. It's been happening for too many years. I can't, I can't, I can't."

What else are you going to do? Suck it up and find him, or go home without him. For twenty minutes, she circled the neighborhood, her nose stuffy and eyes raw with tears. The empty streets showed no sign of her husband; it was time to check hotels. The only parking available was in the darkest, dankest lots, so she stopped the car in a tow-away zone in front of the Marriott.

Allison weighed heavy in her arms by the time she approached the front desk. A sullen ache spanned across the small of Kimberley's back, and her head pounded, a combination of dehydration and surging hormones.

"Did Brennan Roderick check in this morning?" She hiked Allison higher on her hip. "It would've been about an hour ago."

The reservations clerk met her gaze and quickly looked back to his computer screen. "I don't recall registering anyone after midnight, but I'll look for you." He tapped the keyboard and shook his head. "No one under that name. I'm sorry."

"Thank you." Her tears intensified and she rested Allison's bottom on the counter.

"Can I do something else to help you? Get you a room?" He glanced out at her car, parked illegally. "A valet, maybe?"

"Can you call the police?"

"The police?" He handed over the receiver and dialed from behind the desk. "I hope everything's all right, ma'am."

The dispatch officer connected her with a sergeant, she relayed the entire fiasco, and the officer replied, "What exactly do you need from me?"

"I need help finding my husband. I have a sleeping three-year-old in my arms, I'm pregnant, and—"

"Look, go home and wait for him to turn up. You're in a reasonably good neighborhood, and—"

"Has anyone matching his description been arrested?"

"Near the riverboat?" The officer chuckled. "A lot of men have been arrested tonight, same as every night out there. Is your husband the type to cause trouble?"

"No, but he's intoxicated, and—"

"Why was he intoxicated?"

"That's the question of my life. My God, if I could answer that, I'd—"

"Ma'am, I'm sorry for your situation, but it is, in fact, your situation. I can't do anything for you."

She hung up the phone, shifted Allison's dead weight, thanked the clerk, and headed back toward the car. Allison awakened when she placed her into her seat. "Mommy? Where are we?"

"We're going home, Allie."

"Why are you crying?"

"I'm not crying." She sniffled, buckled her in, and began to settle into the front seat, when suddenly, out of the corner of her eye, she saw Brennan.

Less than a block away, he wandered aimlessly, looking both exhausted and irate, with half-closed eyes.

"Bren!" She drove toward him, and before long, he spotted the car. "Brennan, thank God."

Reeking of whiskey and with ice-cold skin, he shoved her hand away. "Lost my cell phone, lost two grand, lost my jacket."

"Daddy."

"Hey, angel pie." Brennan's drunken, glassy gaze shifted to Kimberley. "You brought Allie? What the fuck were you thinking?"

"What was I supposed to do with her, Bren?"

They spent the ride home in silence, save the occasional serenade of the music box embedded in Pink. Once parked in the first stall, Kimberley and Brennan simultaneously opened the back doors to retrieve their daughter. "I'll get her," she said.

"I can do it, Kimmy Coco Bop."

"No, you can't. You can't even walk right now."

"I'm fine. I can—"

"Don't you touch her."

He glared at her before slamming the car door and turning away.

Her arms laden, she managed to open the mudroom door. Two seconds later, the motor of Brennan's luxury sedan turned over, and before she could stop him, he drove away.

Not fifteen minutes later, he announced his return with a crash.

* * *

"I thought you'd be asleep by now." Diane pulled a unisex T-shirt from her braless torso and tossed it into the hamper.

The rare sight of her body—though only a shadow of what it used to be—tantalized Luke from the inside out. "Diane," he whispered.

She stepped out of today's sweatpants. Grey, stained with grape jelly. Her bony rear beckoned, calling for him to reach for her, pull the briefs from her body, and get her from behind.

In high school, she'd leaned over the hood of his car in Rutger's cornfield. He'd pulled her skirt up behind her, yanked aside her imitation silk panties, and they'd done it so fucking well, her ass grinding against his thighs.

"Diane."

"Oh, please. Do we have to go through this every night?"

"Do you love me?"

She shook her head. "You make the concession this time. You could've had your way last time."

"What, if I'd forced you?"

"Yes."

"Do you love me?"

She yanked a jersey-type nightgown over her head. "I don't think so." She plopped into bed, turned her back to him, and reached for this week's book, *The White Knight*, a heaving-breasted woman in the arms of a man with a rippling chest on the front cover.

"When did it happen?"

"What?"

"When did you stop loving me?"

"I don't know that I've ever loved you."

"That's not true."

"No?"

"If it is…why? Why do we sleep in the same bed? Why do we come home to the same house?"

She dropped her book onto the nightstand and turned toward him. "Why do you always come back? Why don't you get it over with? And stay gone?"

He moistened his lips and pulled her tight to his chest. Limp, she was the usual rag doll in his arms. Still, it felt good to hold her, to kiss her stiff, unresponsive mouth, stale from hours of sleep in the family room.

"Just hurry, okay?" she whispered. "Please."

"I want you to want it. Can I just…can I try to help you want it?"

He raised a hand to a breast. "You used to like this."

"Don't remind me of mistakes I've made."

"You used to put my hands here on your own."

"Before two children shriveled me to raisins."

"They're still here. Nicer than they used to be."

"Give me a break, will you?"

"Try, Diane. Please. It'll feel good if you let yourself try. What can I do to help? To help you want it?"

"Nothing. I don't want it."

"Do you want it from Rachael's father?"

"Oh, for heaven's sake." She rolled away.

The slim contour of her body remained against his hands, imprinting, but fading fast. "We should talk about this."

"We've been talking about it since she was born, Luke, and I can't put it any plainer for you. She's yours now, that's all that matters, and that was your decision, not mine. You didn't have to come back, you know."

"Yes, I did."

"For who, Luke? You didn't come back for me. You came back for Caleb."

His cell phone rang from the pile of dirty clothes on the floor.

"Who the hell is calling you at this hour?"

"I don't know."

"Go ahead and answer it." Diane retrieved her book. "We're done anyway."

Numb from head to toe, he reached to the floor. The ringing had stopped, but he picked up the phone, checking the Caller ID screen.

It was Kimberley.

CHAPTER 7

"Kimmy?"

She opened her tired eyes to find her husband leaning over her, rubbing her stomach under her cotton nightgown. A small sense of satisfaction darted through her, knowing yesterday Luke had seen her body through it.

She closed her eyes again, remembering the fire in his eyes when he'd observed her through the window, the sound of his soft gasp the exact second she'd bent over.

"Kimmy, I—"

"Don't tell me you're sorry." She shook him away with a piercing glare.

He reached out for her. "I don't know what happened. One minute I was at a black-jack table, and the next I was—"

"You don't have to tell me. I remember what happened."

"Kimmy."

"It's bad enough you'd put me in that situation, Brennan, but Allie?"

"I didn't ask you to come get me last night."

"No, you told me to."

"I could've called a cab."

"Then why did you call me? Why did you bully me into driving down to Elgin, to the Riverboat district—"

"I don't know. I don't remember. I'm sorry."

"Do you think I honestly care that you're sorry? The little girl down the hall is old enough to remember now. She's growing up, not that you've been around to see it, and she's big enough to know when things are wrong."

"I know. I'm sorry."

"How many times are you going to be sorry for the same damn thing? Sorry doesn't work anymore. You need to get a handle on this. Love me, love Allie enough to control yourself."

"Do you think I don't try? I swear to you, I do."

"I'm tired of your trying, Brennan."

His hand wandered to her breasts.

If she closed her eyes and pretended the hand were callused and scarred, like Luke's, it felt nice. Comforting.

The telephone rang, and she answered it, thankful for an excuse to roll away. "Hello."

"Hi, beautiful girl."

Her heart pounded, while Brennan rubbed her back. "Hi."

"I tried your cell, but you didn't answer. Is he there?"

"Yes."

"Are you okay?"

"Yes."

"Can you meet me in an hour?"

"Yes."

"Say 'no, thank you,' and hang up the phone. I'll see you soon."

"No, thank you." She hung up the phone.

*   *   *

"He did what?" Luke asked, walking alongside Kimberley on the forest preserve jogging path.

"He drove directly into the third stall door."

"Is he all right?"

"Yeah, he's fine, and surprisingly, so is the car, but the garage door needs some work. I suppose it's better he hit the garage, instead of the ragtop parked inside, but now I have to call for service. It's going to look like I did it."

"Why do you think that?"

"Because I'm a woman aiming a big vehicle at a narrow stall door."

"Oh, don't worry about that old stereotype. Believe it or not, most repairmen don't give a hoot about the circumstance, as long as you pay your bill."

"I'm just glad he didn't hurt himself, but it's only a matter of time before he does something a repairman can't fix."

He tossed a blanket onto the ground at the site they now referred to as their place. "Have a seat."

"Thanks." She kicked off her sandals and emptied a bag of pedicure tools and lotions. "I don't even know who to call to fix it."

"Jackson's. I'll give you the number."

"Thanks. That'll help."

"So, about these beautiful breasts..."

She smiled, blinking up at him through the sunshine. "What about them?"

"Are you going to breastfeed?"

"For the last time, that's none of your business."

"Tell me you are, and I'll shut up about it." He daringly reached for her left breast and dragged a finger along its contour.

She stared hard into his eyes, hoping her pleasure was not nearly as noticeable as it felt in her flushing cheeks. "Don't do that again."

"I can't help it."

"I mean it."

"After Friday in the rain... Jesus, Kimber, they're perfect."

Friday in the rain was undoubtedly the best part of that day. And it could have been even better, had she invited Luke to join her inside.

She grabbed an exfoliating lotion, yet before she opened it, Luke stole it from her hands.

"I'm good at this part." He squeezed a dollop into his palm and pulled her feet into his lap. "Besides, pregnant women should have their feet massaged daily."

She probably should have protested, but his rough hands worked her aching feet with such perfection she didn't have it in her to deny him.

"It helps with circulation. My wife's ankles never swelled during pregnancy." His brown eyes punctuated his statement. "Never."

"I didn't know such a thing was possible. When I was pregnant with Allison, my ankles were huge." She looked away. "As was the rest of me."

"If you were my wife, I'd wake you like this every morning."

"Would you fuck me afterward?"

A long, slow smile crept into his eyes before appearing in his lips. "I don't fuck, but yeah. I think I'd find my way inside you."

"What about the pure and true glow of pregnancy?"

"There's nothing in the world more stimulating. I have a thing for pregnant women. That's when I felt closest to my wife. When she was pregnant with Caleb. That's why it hurt so bad when she wouldn't touch me."

His hands worked the lotion around her feet, his thumbs pressing hard along her arches. "You're good at what you do."

"You have no idea. And breastfeeding's important, Kim. If you were my wife, I'd make damn sure that baby was nursed."

"And I'd make damn sure you were up in the middle of the night to keep me company."

"Oh, we'd be up in the middle of the night, for sure. Doing all the things I can't do to you now."

"It's a good thing I'm not your wife. We might never leave the bedroom."

"You say that like it's a bad thing."

"Who'd take care of the children?"

"You'd have my children?" he asked with a coy smile. "I'll take that as a compliment."

"This is a crazy conversation. I'm not your wife."

"Oh, I know what you aren't, but what I can't figure out is what you are."

"I'm a woman who shouldn't be here." She slid her feet out from under his hands and tossed him a towel. "I'm a woman who shouldn't let those hands anywhere near me."

"But you want to, don't you?" He swiped the towel against his thick, rough, amazing hands.

"It doesn't matter what I want. I'm married, and I'm pregnant."

"So now's the best time. There's one thing you can't get before that baby's born, and that's pregnant again."

"Let's not talk about it. I mean, really, Luke, what would Diane do if she knew you'd just invited me into your bed?"

"Nothing. That's not the way she works. She'd make life so insanely miserable I'd want to leave. She knows I won't. She knows I promised Caleb, but—"

"So why risk it?"

"Because I need more. And so do you."

"You don't even know me, and you're willing to risk your marriage, your children."

"You're incredible." He reached for and massaged a foot. "Your husband doesn't know how good he's got it, but I know, Kimberley. I think about you everyday, and I know."

Luke wasn't touching more than her feet, but she felt his hands everywhere. In her mind, they were entwined, and he was inside her, moving like Jason.

Luke crawled toward her, as if he'd just spun a bottle in a circle of teenage friends. He leaned over her, parting his lips.

An inch of air hovered between them.

When she backed away, he only leaned closer, compelling her onto her back.

"Think of the consequence." Her words were a breathy dare: *Kiss me.* "Don't do it, Luke. I'm not worth it."

"Don't do what?" He chuckled. "I'm not touching you. I just want to know what it feels like to be above you."

It felt great to be under him. "Promise me."

"Anything."

"Thank you."

"What am I promising?" He flashed his smile.

"Don't kiss me."

"I only want..." He took a deep breath. "...to inhale you."

Was he as biologically as ready as she? With her hand a millimeter away from investigating, she came to her senses just in time and scrambled out from under him. She might have kicked his shin.

"What now?" He sat back on a heel, like a catcher behind home plate.

"Tell me about your wife."

"What about her?"

"I don't know." She reached for an emery board and filed her toenails. "Just tell me something about her."

"What are you doing?"

"Fulfilling my alibi. My toes."

The same finger that trailed along her left breast caressed a tiny patch of bare skin on her side, just above her hip, where her T-shirt pulled away from her body.

She glanced up at his intense eyes. "Can you sit here without touching me?"

"I don't think so."

"Try."

"You're just so pretty."

"Is Diane pretty?"

He nodded, and his hand came to rest against her abdomen. "Yeah."

"Do you love her?"

"Yeah."

"If that's true, why are you here?"

"Why are you here?" He frowned and snapped his hand away. "I'm not here alone, you know. It wasn't my idea to bend over in a soaking wet nightie. I'd rather not see your hair curling in the rain at all, rather not see your name light up my telephone at three in the morning. My God, do you think this is easy for me?"

Her mouth fell open.

"If you feel superior to assume this attraction is all on my side of the fence, that's fine," he said. "But let me know the rules before we start playing the game."

"The point is, Luke, that we shouldn't play a game together at all."

"Great. Go home and wait for your husband to realize what he has in you, and hope he doesn't gamble away your future in the mean time."

She stopped filing. "What did you say?"

He winced. "I'm sorry. I shouldn't—"

"You don't know my husband."

"Do I need to?"

"He gives me everything he can."

"He gives you a whopping headache."

Well, he was right about that.

"Look." Luke waved away an insect. "You're taken care of, and I guess that's something, but would you stay with him if the security weren't there?"

Would she?

"He might lose everything someday. Would you still be there, if he did?"

"We're both adults here. We can control ourselves, can't we?"

"That depends. Can your husband control himself? Was he controlling himself last night when he demanded you bring your sick little girl to the riverboat district to find him? Was he controlling himself when he went for a drive and then crashed into your garage? Control is all a matter of relativity. It's *quid pro quo*."

"My husband has addictions." She applied cuticle softener, her hands as steady as steel. "And he's unfaithful, I'll give you that much. But my husband craves the rush of a game and the company of No. 7, not an extra-marital skirt."

"How do you know? How do you know he doesn't wager oral sex? How do you know he doesn't bet his buddies who can get into the bartender's pants the fastest? *Quid pro quo*, Kimber."

"There's nothing *quid pro quo* about this."

"It doesn't matter how he's doing it. With or without the bartender's panties, by your own definition, he's still cheating on you."

"So you want me to give him a taste of his own medicine? But instead of betting a paycheck, I should bet my marriage? Instead of drinking whiskey when it all falls apart, I should drink you?"

"Maybe."

She began to shake her head.

"Do you swallow?"

"I beg your pardon?"

"Swallow. Do you?"

"Yes." Why had she answered in the affirmative? She and Jason had used oral sex as foreplay. Ejaculating into her mouth, according to Jason, would be impolite, unromantic, and unnecessary.

And as far as Brennan was concerned, he was usually too drunk to finish fellatio.

"I want to taste you, beautiful girl." Luke inched toward her, crawling between her legs. "I'm harmless." He maneuvered around her bent knee and rested his head in her lap. "I can't lose my children, but if there were a way we wouldn't get caught—and I mean an airtight, sure-as-death way—I'd be all over you. Would you wake me with a blowjob? Would you swallow me?"

One of his hands cupped her backside. She said nothing, simply reached beyond the bulk of his body for a bottle of burgundy organza nail polish. She imagined seeing Brennan's mouth only inches from some woman's crotch and shuddered at the mental picture. But she couldn't push Luke away.

"I wish you knew," Luke said. "I wish you understood."

"Understood what?" She pretended not to notice the brushing of his lips against her inner thigh, the trailing of his fingers along her hip.

"That we're soul mates, beautiful girl. I wish you could feel it."

The pressure of his mouth intensified, deepening her breaths to uneven, erratic inhalations. *I'll give you something to feel. Stick that hot tongue inside me.*

She closed her eyes, imagining those pouting lips gently massaging her clitoris, that pink tongue swirling against her from the inside out, his head bobbing between her pregnant thighs, and—

"Or maybe you can. Can you feel it?"

Yes, Luke, I can feel it, I love it, I want it. "It doesn't matter what I want. I can't indulge."

"Let me make love to you."

"You want to fuck me. Let's not confuse the issue."

"I'm not confused."

She painted her toenails, the rapid beat of her heart reverberating in her ears. Luke equated sex, inside and out. And when she was with him, so did she.

"It might not make sense right now," Luke said. "But try not to think about it. Just follow what feels natural. We all have needs, don't we?"

"Yes."

"I know what I need. And you know what you need, too. Don't you?"

"Yes."

"I shouldn't have to beg for intimacy, should I? She should want it, too, right?"

"I think so."

"And don't even get me started about what should be happening between your legs. If you were mine, you'd be on fire from the friction. You wouldn't be waiting at home for contact with a man too drunk to remember who he dropped a grand on the night before."

She dropped the polish brush back into the bottle and ran her free hand through his silky hair. He was right. She deserved a man who wanted to love her properly, and Luke deserved a woman who loved him, period.

"That feels good," he said.

It certainly did.

"We all have needs," he said again. "Diane doesn't meet mine, and Brennan... Hell, he doesn't even know how fragile his situation is. He's got the greatest thing in the world waiting at home for him, and if he doesn't get there soon..."

She'd do something that would turn her life upside down. She'd cross the line Brennan drew in the sand the day he uttered, "Family-shmamily."

Luke's lips parted against her, and softly, he kissed her inner thigh.

Heaven.

Wrong.

"We shouldn't." She attempted to pry his hands off her body, taking care not to spill the nail polish.

"Aren't you tired of doing the right thing?" he asked, his amazing biceps tightening against her thighs.

"I can't afford to tire." She continued to pull at his hands. "And neither can you."

"I'll tell you what I'm tired of. I'm tired of not feeling wanted. I'm tired of Diane refusing to kiss me, let alone sleep with me. I'm tired of whacking off in the shower."

The mental picture consumed her—Luke, soaking wet, in the act of self-gratification. "Oh, God," she whispered.

His hand pressed against her backside, and she straightened. "I'll ask one more time. Get off me."

He obeyed. Amid a sudden silence, she tended to a second coat of nail polish, refusing to raise her eyes to his. He was probably pouting those full, supple lips at her, and if she looked, she'd want to bite into his mouth.

She glanced anyway.

He rubbed his eyes with the thumb and middle finger of his left hand, looking tired, spent, and dissatisfied.

"I'm sorry, Luke, but—"

"It's not your fault."

"But I'm using you."

"What?"

"I'm using you. My husband may shake away a long, hard week at a sports bar. But I'm getting my fill of the devil with you."

"You want me to fill you with the devil?" Luke smiled. "You call this sinning? Because in your mind we're already doing it?"

"In my mind, we've already done it hundreds of times. Being with you is like being with Jason."

"Does Brennan know how you still feel about Jason?"

"I don't even know how I feel about Jason."

"You're hopelessly obsessed with him."

"I am not."

"Yes, you are." Luke lay on his back, five inches from her pedicure, smiling full force. His blazing white teeth seem to illuminate the air.

"Luke, I assure you I'm not obsessed with my ex-boyfriend. I'm fixated on knowing that, once, I was a priority for a man, and that, once, I was truly loved. And now..." A lump formed in her throat and tears gathered on her lashes. *Hormones.*

"Now, what?"

It was such an absurd truth anyway. Did she have to admit it? Couldn't she continue to ignore it?

He brushed a tear from her cheek. "Kimberley?"

"Now I'm a birthing vehicle that holds less priority than a job he hates. I'm not as important than his friends, his games, or his highball glass, and I don't understand why." Although her bawling had become hysterical, she continued with her pedicure, tightly capping the nail color and opening a bottle of quick drying topcoat. "And until he does something monumentally stupid, until he loses our house, or maybe his life, I'm supposed to be okay with things. I'm supposed to turn away."

With one steady movement, Luke stabilized her closest, shaking hand and pulled the tiny bottle from her fingers.

Luke's stare sizzled through her. "Relax."

"I don't want to relax. I want to be loved the way I deserve to be loved. I don't want to deal with repairing the garage door, hoping he doesn't kill someone on his way home from a bar, hoping he doesn't drink himself into a coma or wager Allie's college fund. I want this baby to be proud of his father."

"Kimber."

"What?"

"He's an addict. You have to give him time."

"Do you want to fuck me, or do you want to save my marriage? Make up your goddamn mind." She wiped tears from her cheeks.

"I know what I want," he said with a straight, serious face. "And I know it's worth the price, but I don't know if we can pay it."

"If you really want me, you'd want to leave her."

"It isn't her...it's my boy. My kids. I stay up at night, wondering why I didn't find you back then, when I was without spouse, without child, and when you were working your way out of the same situation I was walking into. Things could've been so much easier for us."

"Why, then, did you find me when things can only be difficult? If we're soul mates, why did your good Lord put us together now? Why not eight years ago?"

"I don't know anything about why I found you when I did, but you're very pretty when you cry." He smiled, touching her on the chin. "We all make choices, Kimber. But someday, we'll realize that choices are like beds. You make them, you sleep in them, roll around in them, try them out for comfort, but eventually, they need to be remade."

"I don't know if I can remake it today. Or next week, or even next year."

He gently peeled her hands from her face. "That's fine, beautiful girl." He stared into her crying eyes, as if he had an eternity to swim in her gaze. "I'll wait."

CHAPTER 8

"Allie, hurry, or we'll be late." Kimberley rinsed the breakfast dishes and glanced at the clock. *Wednesday.* Ballet day, errand day, and laundry day—the busiest day of the week.

Allison, dressed in the third leotard she'd tried on that day and with a full bun atop her head, scampered into the kitchen. She wore a light jacket and gym shoes. "I can't find Pink."

"What do you mean, you can't find him? He never leaves your hand."

"He's gone."

Great. Already five minutes after departure time, and they had to search the monstrous house for a beat-up rabbit Allison couldn't even bring into the studio. "Where did you last see him?"

"In the potty. When I went."

"Did you look there?"

"Yes. He's gone, Mommy."

Kimberley dried her hands. "I'm sure he isn't gone."

A look of distress crossed the three-year-old's face. "Yes, he is. He's gone forever."

"Baby, I'm sure he's here somewhere." But after searching Allison's bedroom, her bathroom, and every square inch along the way to the kitchen, Kimberley still had not found him. "We'll have to look when we get home, Allie. We're late."

"No!"

"Allie, come on. I'm sure he's here, he's just—"

"Kim?" Elsie, Wednesday's hired help, appeared in the breakfast room.

"I know, I know," Kimberley said. "I'm low on dryer sheets and color safe bleach. I'll pick some up on the way home."

"He's gone forever?" Allison wiped a hand over her cheeks, her eyes a stinging violet blue, much brighter with tears.

"Kim?"

"What, already?" Kimberley shoved an annoying, stray curl off her forehead and turned to her grandmotherly maid, who was holding the rabbit in question. "Oh, I'm sorry, Elsie. I'm nauseous, we're so late, and—"

"Someone likes the laundry basket." Elsie smiled and danced the rabbit over to a much-relieved Allison, who giggled and squeezed the stuffed animal tight to her chest.

"I want my other dance clothes, Mommy."

"Thanks, Elsie. And no, Allie, we're late."

"I want to wear my pink ones, not my black ones."

"We don't have time."

"But I don't like these tights."

"Get out to the car." She opened the mudroom door, and a complaining Allison stepped into the garage.

With the touch of a button, the first stall door opened, and a beam of bright sunshine darted into the dim space. "Bright, Mommy. I need my sunglasses."

"They're in the car." Kimberley slid her sunglasses from their post at her head to the bridge of her nose.

"No, I want my purple ones, and they're in on my vanity. I'll go in and get them. They're—"

"Allison Colleen, get in the car!"

"Who's that?" Allison asked, stopping in her tracks.

With a stutter-step, Kimberley avoided knocking her daughter over, peered over her Wayfarers, and spied a black pick-up truck parked in the driveway.

"'Morning, Mrs. Roderick," Luke said with a smile.

"That's a repairman, Allie. Get in the car, or we'll be late."

"A repairman for what?"

"The garage...now get in the car."

"What happened to the garage?"

"Allie, please."

"Okay." Allison dutifully climbed into her car seat and began to fasten the buckle, while her mother approached the man in her driveway.

He whistled. "Cute kid. Kind of feisty. Does she get that from her mother?"

"What are you doing here?"

"Measuring. You need a new panel, but you don't have to replace the whole door."

She glanced over her shoulder. Allison was nearly settled. "So who hired you to do it?"

"Look, I'd appreciate the work." He pressed a business card into her hand. "You said you needed it done, so here I am."

"Jackson's Home Services," she read off the card. "Lucas K. Jackson, President." She eyed him over her glasses. "Very amusing, Luke," she said. *Never let him see your emotion. Never let him know what you're thinking.*

"So, do you want me to do it? Or don't you?"

"Yeah. Go ahead and do it."

"Think of something else for me to do on my lunch break, will you?" He laughed as she walked away.

* * *

"You look exhausted," Lauren said.

Kimberley sank to the chair next to her best friend's outside the ballet studio. "I am, honey. With Allie's unstoppable energy, and Brennan's being out of town all week, and now he's been staying over Thursdays…" She sighed and shook her head. "I don't mean to complain, but the first trimester is always the hardest."

"How's Bren?"

"He seems worse lately. Spending more, drinking more." She studied the ring on her finger. "Has he always been this bad? Or am I exaggerating the issue because I'm pregnant and irrational?"

"Honey, has he lost more than you can afford?"

"Not yet, but—"

"Then don't worry. Use it to your advantage. When he loses eight hundred, it's a pair of Blahniks and a Kate Spade for you."

"But it's only a matter of time, and you should see the way's been coming home lately. Drunker than drunk."

"He's always been responsible with his drinking, Kimmy. He's been working triple duty. He's probably blowing off steam. It'll pass."

"He doesn't want anyone to know this, but he drove into the garage door last weekend."

"You know, he swears he always calls a cab."

"Well, he doesn't." The rest of the story, about her trek to Elgin, hopped onto the tip of Kimberley's tongue, but wives like her gossiped only about their husbands' trivial downfalls, such as his failure to lower the toilet seat or neglecting to put a pair of boxers into the hamper. Wives like her saved the ugly, torrential problems for the private confines of their own homes, and she'd already said too much.

Lauren placed a hand upon hers. "Go home. Take a bubble bath. Not a hot bath—think of the baby—but go jump in the tub. I'll keep Allie for the afternoon. Go."

While the uncontrollable pulse within her pleaded to be alone with Luke, the rational side of her put a damper on the thought. She had no business seeing him on a one-on-one basis in such an intimate setting, only four walls away from five beds inside an empty house. "That's not necessary. I'll be all right."

"Will you go? You're forgetting I'm the one woman who understands exactly what it feels like to endure an on-a-roll-and-smashed-out-of-his-gourd Brennan Roderick. You know, he would never scale down his gambling for me, Kimmy, but he's done that for you. And you're carrying another child for him, so take a few hours for yourself. Here." She fished through her wallet and produced a coupon for bath salts. "Stop at Lyndi's and pick up a little something special for yourself. Two-for-one."

* * *

Luke was gone when she returned from the ballet studio. Both disappointed and relieved, she made her way to the master bedroom, bumping into Elsie and a basket of dirty laundry along the way.

Elsie gave Kimberley a nod. "Did you remember bleach?"

"No, but wait a minute." She raised a finger, slipped out of her clothes, and tossed them into the basket. "I think I'm already gaining weight. Nothing fits."

"You could stand to gain some. No one eats anymore." Elsie carried on down the hallway. "I won't use bleach then."

Kimberley closed the door and paused before a full-length mirror. *I look incredible.* Her figure rivaled that of Jason's hourglass, and her hair seemed uncharacteristically tame. She cupped her full, tender breasts, rubbing her thumbs over her nipples. Her breasts, thanks to pregnancy, were amazing. Not large enough to lift to her mouth, but heavy and round. Made for Luke's lips.

She donned a short-sleeved, thigh-length, silk robe and grabbed the cordless telephone and a favorite novel. Maybe she'd actually finish reading it this spring, unlike all previous years of motherhood. With one of Allison's satin-trimmed blankets tucked under her arm, she headed out to the back yard and settled into a hammock in her underwear, feeling carefree.

Although no one seemed to be golfing today, their home was the hub of a two-acre lot off the ninth green. At any moment, a neighbor might tee off on the back nine and see her. Daring, provocative, sexy.

And nauseous.

She closed her eyes, rested her head upon her daughter's blanket, and waited for the surge of queasiness to pass.

Just think of something else.

Had she married Jason, would she be satisfied with her marriage? Would she be tempted to stray? Had the hourglass ever strayed? Did she know she had a goldmine of a man? Jason's lovemaking—so tender, so deep—would be enough to keep any woman, under any circumstances, safe at home.

While sex with Jason was never backward, sideways, standing, or upside down, it was always sober, hands-in-her-hair-while-he-kissed-her, romantic.

Over the past eight years, she'd been laid without being kissed at all. That fact once riveted her, but suddenly, it disturbed her. Why didn't her husband take the time to lose his hands in her hair?

* * *

"Kimberley?"

"Yeah." Her pretty, green eyes flickered open, and she yawned a breathy yawn.

"Did you sleep well, beautiful girl?" From his position on the ground next to the hammock, Luke caressed her bare abdomen—such soft skin—between the folds of the sexiest robe he'd seen since he'd caught a glimpse at a Victoria's Secret flyer. "I'll be back Thursday to stain it. But there you have it—one bona fide, cherry panel garage door."

"So you're a fix-it man."

"Trim carpentry, cabinetry, that sort of thing."

"I thought you were a plumber. Or an electrician."

"I'm surprised a woman like you knows the difference. A

tradesman is a tradesman, right?"

"I wouldn't say that I'd—"

"I know how to wire, and I know my way around a faucet, too." He flattened his hand against her and let out a guttural groan. God, touching her this way was going to—

"Anything else you know your way around?"

"I plow in the winter, too, if you're in need." He grazed his fingers against her bare skin. "You're skin is so smooth, so—" He lost eye contact; they both looked to his hand.

"Oh!" She gasped, pulling at her open robe. "I'm sorry, I—"

"Aw, don't do that," he whispered.

"I didn't mean for—"

"Let me look at you. Please."

And remarkably, her hands stilled, one falling atop his. She licked her lips. "You were gone, so I thought—"

"Hmm." He raked his gaze over her lacey bra, down to her delicate panties, all the while sweeping his hand in a small circle against her pelvis. "You're so pretty."

"Thank you."

"God, you have no idea. You don't know you're beautiful." His gaze simmered, locking on her emerald eyes. "Where's your daughter?"

"Ballet class."

"Where's your bedroom?"

Her lower lip seceded from its upper counterpart.

"Which window, I mean. Is it in the turret?"

"How did you know that?"

"I want you in that window at three in the morning."

She nodded. "All right."

And if he isn't home, give me the nod, and I'll come up. Luke rose from his position before he gathered the nerve to voice his thoughts. "I should go."

"Wait. What do I owe you?"

"A glass of water."

"No, really."

"Really." He licked his lips. "A glass of water." He unfastened and removed his tool belt and looked to his truck, where he knew he ought to be heading.

"Come on in." She rolled from the hammock and tightened the sash around her waist.

Who could resist an invitation coming from this woman?

"Gorgeous place," he said, following her into her home. He deposited his tool belt on the floor and sat on an upholstered settee. The springs creaked.

She waltzed into the kitchen and selected a glass from a custom cabinet. "You know that's really just for show. It can't be too comfortable."

"What, this?" Luke shifted on the tiny sofa. "It's fine." But it was far from it. Still, the view of the kitchen—and the woman moving like music through it—was worth the discomfort.

"I sit there sometimes," she said. "But it isn't even comfortable for me." She placed a glass of water, along with a bowl of fresh, green grapes, onto a serving tray and headed toward the monstrous great room, hitching her chin in invitation. "Come on."

He followed her into the sunken living space, easily a third the size of his entire home, and, with its cathedral ceiling, it seemed even larger. When she bent to position the tray onto an oversized, cushioned ottoman, he caught a glimpse of her curvaceous rear, cheeks peeking out from lace-trimmed panties. Someday, he'd get her from behind.

She eased onto the sofa, feet tucked under her. Although he estimated seating for twelve in the gigantic room, he chose to sit immediately to her right. Dangerously close.

"So, how are you?" He popped a grape into his mouth.

Her lips parted and closed without a word, as if in debate about what to admit. She glanced away. "I'm fine."

"How's Brennan?"

"According to my best friend, he's better than he's ever been, but considering your work order today, all evidence is to the contrary."

"And you're fine with that."

Her beautifully manicured hands tugged at the hemline of her robe. "Not really."

"So, how are you?"

"How's Diane?"

"I think I touched you more today than I've touched her in months. Is this Allie?" He reached across her, his forearm grazing against her bosom, and retrieved a framed portrait from an end table. "She's a pretty little girl, like her mama."

"Thank you, but I think she looks like Brennan."

He licked his suddenly dry lips and stared at her. "I don't cheat on my wife—"

"Are you trying to convince me, or yourself?" She took the frame from his hands and put it back on the table.

"—but I want to see you, with nothing on, lying in bed, waiting for me."

"Why don't you admit what you really want? You don't have to sugar coat the situation. Hinging upon the conversations we've shared, you don't have to be polite. You don't want to make love to me, you don't want to lay me down in rose petals. You don't care that I'm pregnant, and you wouldn't care if I happened to be a virgin. You want to fuck me, plain and simple."

"Fine, I want to fuck you. Is that what you want to hear? Did it ever occur to you that I might not be sugar coating the situation for your benefit, but that I *do* want to lay you down in rose petals?"

"Lust is in no way particular about its object."

"I don't think you're an object."

"Well, I certainly doubt you think I'm an angel with the answers to your daily prayers in the palm of my hand."

"Is it so hard to believe you're wonderful?"

"This conversation is moot. Say I did leave my husband. You're hardly in any position to take his place, and you don't want to."

"We can get custody of my kids. You said—"

"You don't know me, Luke. And you don't want to know me. Not like that anyway."

He cocked his head, staring at her belly, and tucked a finger under the sash of her robe. He yanked it open and smoothed his hand over her midsection. "When do you go to listen for the baby's heartbeat?"

"A few weeks."

"Can I go with you?"

"Why?"

"I want to. Hearing the heartbeat for the first time is something every woman should share with a certain, special someone, and I dare say your husband won't be there with you." He pulled her close, feeling her breath on his cheek. Beneath the robe, his hands trailed to her back. "You have the softest skin, beautiful girl."

"This is wrong," she whispered.

"But it feels good." He closed his eyes, concentrating on the feel of her breasts against his chest, her cheek brushing against his, her lips feathering a kiss at his ear. He breathed deeply, swallowing the scent of her hair. Floral, not fruity. Expensive. Hard on the pocketbook, easy on the senses. "Kimberley."

"Yes."

"I have to go." He began to withdraw.

"You don't have to go." But she didn't pull him back for more.

"Yeah, I do. Julie's got my dog, and I should probably—"

"Your sister?"

"And I want to go see my boy." With one last caress on her thigh, he rose from the sofa and exited, taking his tool belt with him.

On the way out of town, he spotted a pink-and-yellow banner in the dance studio window, advertising a spring ballet recital. While Allison Roderick practiced in that studio for the big event, he'd nearly made love to her mother.

God, he'd come close. He wouldn't be able to stop himself next time. But as much as he wanted her, he couldn't risk losing his children. Perhaps next time should be out of the question.

* * *

"Hey, Caleb." Luke entered the kitchen, Derby at his heels.

Caleb didn't take his eyes from his video game in the next room. "Hey, Dad."

Diane stood at the stove, stirring macaroni and cheese.

"Hi, Diane."

"How was counseling?" she asked, refusing to turn around.

"Fine."

"Dr. Schaeffer called. You didn't show."

"You caught me. I didn't go."

"So where were you?"

"Not that you care, but I went to a jobsite." He meandered to the sink and closed his eyes for a few moments, savoring the memory of Kimberley's body in his arms. He pretended to scratch his nose, inhaling the scent of her from his fingers one last time before washing it off.

"Rachael, lunch!" Diane called. "Caleb, come on."

"I've got three guys left, Mom."

"Come on, Caleb," Luke said. "Put it on pause."

Diane shot daggers in his direction, as if the discipline of their son was not his business.

"What's for lunch?" Luke asked.

"I didn't know you'd be home, so I didn't plan anything for you. Make yourself a sandwich."

"You want one?" He opened the refrigerator.

"No."

He peered into the recently stocked meat drawer. One thing about Diane: she knew how to keep a house and how to feed her family. He assembled two large sandwiches, and they gathered at the table, the kids eating cinnamon rolls and macaroni and cheese, Diane sipping a cup of coffee.

"Rachael," Luke said, "would you like to go to a show in a few weeks?"

"Can I come?" Caleb asked.

"If you want. But I thought Rachael might want to go."

"Is Mommy coming?" Rachael asked.

Diane shook her head. "I don't think so."

His girl shrugged. "What kind of show is it?"

"It's little girls your age, dancing."

"Can Mommy take me?"

"I want to take you."

"We'll see, all right, Luke?" Diane said.

CHAPTER 9

"It looks great." Brennan studied the third stall door. He popped an aspirin and washed it down with beer. "Who did it?"

"Jackson's. The guy gave me his card." Nervousness fluttered through Kimberley's stomach with the pretense Luke was just a random repairman.

"Did he say when he was going to stain it?"

"Um, Thursday. I think." Two days ago, actually, but he hadn't shown up and he wasn't at the gym this morning. "I'll call him Monday."

"How much did he charge?"

A glass of water. "A few hundred."

"I'm thinking of renovating the bar," Brennan said.

"Why?"

He shrugged and popped another aspirin. "I had a bit of luck this week."

"Do I want to know?"

"You should." He grinned. "Fifteen grand in the black."

"Fifteen *grand*?"

"I took a detour to Atlantic City, and—"

"What if we'd lost it?"

"Well, I didn't, did I?" He nodded toward the garage. "Does this guy do interior work?"

"I can think of twenty other ways I'd like to spend the money than to renovate a room barely old enough to have acquired a layer of dust."

"I didn't ask you."

"I'd like to get the boat out of the fourth stall and into a marina. I'd like to finish the bonus room. A ballet studio for Allison would be very charming, and don't forget, we have a nursery to furnish."

"When you earn the money, you can allot it as you wish."

"How am I supposed to earn, when you won't let me out of here?"

"Oh, don't be dramatic, Kimmy."

"I want to teach in the fall."

"I thought we decided against that."

"No, you decided against it."

"No, Kimmy, we agreed when we got married. When children came—and they're here now—you raise them. I didn't want kids so some *au pair* could tuck them in at night."

"It would be two days a week. Lauren said she'd take Allie—"

"The welfare of my children is not up for discussion. They'll be best taken care of by you. At home."

"Do you love me?"

Brennan shook his head. "That's a ridiculous question."

"I'm not happy, Brennan."

Laughter hissed through his teeth. "You're spoiled beyond reason. I'm not listening to this." He turned away. "Rick and Lauren are dropping by this afternoon. His sister's in town, and she offered to sit with the kids while we barbeque."

"I mean it, Bren."

"So I thought we'd whip up some filet, maybe some salmon or lobster. Have a few cocktails, wager on some horseshoes—"

"I'm not happy, Brennan!"

He was silent, but only for a second. "You're free to leave."

She followed him into the screened porch.

"Go ahead, Kimmy. If you've got it so rough, go."

"I don't want to go." She grasped his hand. "I want this to work."

He stared at their entwined hands for a moment. Slowly, his gaze traveled to hers.

"I love you, Brennan. But I can't compete with your addictions. You can't get enough of anything—except me."

"That's a crock."

"Is it? You don't even look at me unless you're fucking me."

"I'm looking at you now."

"Working long hours, gambling, drinking. The uneven monetary balance between us, the lack of respect and purpose…it has to change.

It has to stop."

His hand twitched in an involuntary movement he referred to as the shakes, a side effect of over-consumption. "I've never gambled more than I can afford to lose."

"I know, but—"

"I used to drink everyday."

"I know."

"And now, it's mostly weekends."

"I can't do this every weekend, Brennan, especially when weekends are all we have."

"It's the long hours and the days on the road keeping us in this house."

"I'd rather have you, Bren. I don't need—"

"Well, I do need it. You knew this about me when you married me. And it's my money. I'll lose it if I want to, but the thrill's in the winning, and I win plenty. Look around you. You don't want for anything here."

"I want you. Why don't you sit down?"

"Don't treat me like a guest in my own home."

"But that's what you are. You're a guest with whom I share my bed two nights a week. You aren't with me, even when you're here."

"I've accepted things about you, like the vacuuming of your uterus—"

"You can't make me feel worse than I already do about that."

"—so it's your turn to accept me. Accept that I'm trying, but this won't go away overnight."

"You use that as an excuse. Trying is different than making progress, Brennan, and you haven't made any in years."

"And your constant bitch, bitch, bitching about it isn't making anything easier."

"That's not fair."

"Do you think it's fair I have to live up to the standard of some ridiculously dense jock who didn't know enough to wrap his dick before he stuck it in?"

She searched his eyes for warmth, compassion, but found only authoritarian power. "I'm done." She stormed into the house, flung her purse over her shoulder, and reached for the rag-top keys.

She rushed up the stairs, lifted her napping daughter and Pink from the bed, and rushed out to the garage.

She drove northbound on Route 294, with the top down, Allison giggling with the wind in her hair in the tiny backseat. "Where are we going, Mommy?"

"Lake Villa, baby."

"What's Lake Villa?"

"It used to be home." But her connection to the tiny town of lake homes and summer resorts had died the moment Jason left her. She hadn't been back since. Not to visit her sisters, not to drive past the home in which she'd grown up. Less than an hour away, but she'd never found the time...or the courage.

She exited on Route 132, driving westward off the tollway. Thick traffic through Gurnee and Lindenhurst confirmed what she'd suspected: the area had grown. Lake Villa was no longer the sleepy town she'd left behind. New subdivisions, renovations of the old lake communities, new businesses...

She drove down Oakwood Lane, stopping before a brick tri-level. A simple home, she'd once deemed it more than enough. She hadn't always lived as extravagantly as she did now. Would she ever be able to live simply again? She stared at the driveway, where Maura had killed her dog.

"Who lives here?" Allison asked.

"I don't know who lives here now, but this is where I lived when I was a little girl."

"When you were my age?"

"Yes. And you have two aunts who lived here with me."

"Auntie Lauren lived with you?"

"No, Allie. I have two sisters, Maura and Kathleen, and they're your aunts."

"Where do they live now?"

Kimberley shook her head and released the break. "I don't know. I haven't talked to them in a very long time." Her childhood home disappeared in the rearview mirror, leaving her to wonder if it was real. Had she imagined a life in Lake Villa? Had she dreamed the falling out with her sisters after her mother's death?

She'd long since forgotten her mother's face, and she'd never remembered her father's. But the images of Kathleen and Maura remained as clear as a holiday memento. They were real, all right, but no longer part of her.

She was young, eighteen, when her mother died. The argument with Kathleen and Maura centered on what her sisters had coined "her share" of the unimpressive estate her mother had left behind. Funny that something she'd never wanted had robbed her of something she'd always desired—closeness with her sisters.

"You can keep it all." She recited the last words she'd spoken to her sisters. "I'll make my own way."

"What, Mommy?" Allison asked.

"Nothing, baby."

Second stop, north side of Cedar Lake. On the bay. Jason had always wanted to buy his parents' practical Tudor, to raise his children in his childhood backyard. Had his dreams come true? The "Devon" on the mailbox wasn't telling any fortunes. Had Gene and Sheila retired? If Kimberley knocked on the door now, would Jason answer, bare-chested and covered in weekend warrior sweat?

"Who lives here, Mommy?"

"I'm not sure. I always hoped this house would be mine someday."

"It's pretty."

"Isn't it? Would you like to live here?"

"With you?"

"Of course, with me."

"And Daddy?"

Well, no. Kimberley wiped tears from her eyes. Brennan would never live in a lake community so far out of the city, would never stoop to living in a modest home like this one.

Life in Lake Villa had continued without her. Jason had married, and probably fathered. Her sisters, with any luck, had followed their dreams and gotten the hell out. Hopefully, they'd found happiness, or whatever it was they were looking for.

"I don't belong here," Kimberley whispered.

"I'm hungry, Mommy."

"You are?" She dabbed at her eyes with a knuckle. "I know just the place. The best peanut butter and jelly in the lakes region."

"What's the lakes region?"

"Where we are. Here. Where I used to be."

She drove around Cedar Lake and parked the car in a gravel lot next to a building in dire need of renovation.

They entered Dot's Place, the aroma of fried fish, Today's Catch, wafting from the greasy kitchen. For nostalgia's sake, Kimberley refused the front booth by the window—Jason had always referred to that table as the Fish Bowl—and slid into the second.

What would have happened had she and Jason met for lunch in this dingy diner just one more time?

What would have happened had he responded differently to her news? "Jason, I'm pregnant."

His smile appeared, slow and nervous. "Really?"

"I don't know what to do."

His thumb working over her knuckles. "We'll work it out."

Working it out had turned out to mean giving her a few days to think about what she wanted. Law school? Or a family?

"Why are you crying, Mommy?"

She wiped a tear. "Because I'm lucky to have you. Do you know you're the best part of Mommy's life? Do you know that?"

"And Daddy's." Allison grinned.

"And Daddy's." If only he'd show it, once in a while. "After lunch, I'm going to take you to all the places I used to go when I was your age."

"Like where?"

"Well, there's a park not far from here with a real caboose. The rest of the train is gone, but the caboose is still there."

Allison's eyes grew large. "Really?"

"Really. And there's a beach with a pier, where we can skip stones, and take off our shoes and wade in the water. And there used to be a horse farm behind the YMCA, too. We'll buy some carrots and feed the horses."

"Real horses?"

"If they're still there."

"Mommy? I like Lake Villa."

"I used to when I was your age, too."

But then her father left. And then her mother died, and she'd lost her sisters, too. When she'd aborted Jason's child, she'd cut the threads that had connected her to the tiny town. She no longer fit there. Maybe she never did.

* * *

At eight-fifteen, Kimberley carried a sleeping Allison into the house.

"Hi, Kimmy."

She jumped at the sound of Lauren's voice and shifted her daughter. "Where's Bren?"

"Out with Rick."

"Figures."

"He's out looking for you."

"What?" She sank to the sofa and laid Allison across her lap.

"I'm not saying he wasn't an asshole this afternoon," Lauren said. "But what were you thinking? You've been gone for over seven hours."

"He's looking for me? Is he…at the track?"

Lauren shook her head and shrugged at the same time. "Who knows by now?"

"Well, I'm home. You can take the car, go home to your kids."

"Honey, was this a hormonal rant? Or are you serious? Are you really ready to leave him over a few side bets and beers?"

"I don't know why he told you that."

"He was out of his mind, Kim, bawling like a baby. What the hell happened?"

Kimberley's heart ached, wishing her husband would show her raw emotion, the way he obviously still did with Lauren. "You know how it is. I'm just pregnant."

"Talk to me, honey."

"You don't want to talk about this."

"Of course I do. Honey, I'm worried about you, about Bren."

"Don't worry."

"Too late."

"Fine, let's talk."

"Let's."

Kimberley chewed her lip for a moment. "When you were with Brennan…" She brushed the sofa cushion, remembering the way Luke had held her there. "…what was he like in bed?"

"I don't know, Kim. He was…I don't know."

"He's an animal when he fucks. Absolutely crazy."

Lauren's brow knit, as if in confusion. "I should go."

"That's fine. You don't have to say anything else. I know. My husband—kinky, dirty, ass-slapping—used to hold you afterward."

Lauren reached for the discarded car keys. "Kimmy, really, this—"

"I know I'm right. I'm good at interrogation. Opposing counsel used to dread me in that courtroom. By God, I was on my way. And this is what I left it for—an addict, who doesn't show me half the respect he shows his ex-girlfriend."

"You left it for that beautiful treasure sleeping in your lap." Lauren opened the door and stepped one foot out. "And don't you forget it."

* * *

"Hey, Kimmy." Brennan stumbled into the bedroom just after three in the morning. "Shit, you came back. Now I owe Rick five hundred bucks."

Sitting on the window seat in the turret, she looked up from her dish of ice cream. "I'm sorry I left like that."

"Love you," he crooned with a smile and half-open eyes.

"I love you, too."

"Love my cock, too? Say it."

She stifled a shudder and set aside her ice cream dish. "I love your cock." There. Like a robot.

"Can you feel it?" he asked, stepping out of his jeans, losing his balance, and thudding to the floor. He pulled himself up to his feet. "Want to?"

"Of course."

"Come feel it." He meandered toward her, reaching into the fly of his boxer shorts, exposing his penis, and touching it to her lower lip.

She turned out the light, led him to bed, and covered the tip of his penis with her lips.

"Mmm." Brennan pulled her hair as she eased him onto his back. "You may be a spoiled, fucking bitch who just lost me half a grand, but you give head like a whore." He yanked again on her hair. "Like a whore."

"And Lauren?" She forced her way out from under his hands and removed her nightgown, her lips brushing against him.

"She's nothing compared to you." He shoved her head back into his lap and fell asleep almost instantly, but she worked religiously until he reached rock-hard. Imagining seven-and-five-eighths of pure man, she climbed on top.

"Can you feel my cock?" Brennan mumbled in his sleep.

She held on tight to the headboard, riding him deep and slow. Working her vaginal muscles against the rod, maneuvering it deeper and deeper, the way she'd learned. The way she used to like it with Jason. What she imagined Luke to be.

* * *

Luke had returned from a late-night drive an hour ago, but he couldn't drift off. Diane slept next to him, and he stared at her in the dim light of their bedroom, remembering the days of glory they'd shared.

The day they'd met, her golden hair had shimmered in the late-summer sunshine, and she had smiled at him, as if she'd been looking for him her entire life. He'd lain her down on the shores of Lake Michigan, burrowing his fingers into her, feeling her passionate response.

God, he'd been crazy about her. If she'd let herself love him, would he love her still?

Tenderly, he touched his wife's cheek, remembering the beauty he once found in her.

She slowly opened her eyes and sighed in discontent.

"I just want to look at you," he whispered. "I won't touch you, I promise."

She rolled away, depositing his hand upon her pillow. "I can feel her on you," she said.

"What?" A flitting glimpse of panic rose in his chest.

"I know you're not thinking of me with that look in your eyes."

"I was thinking of the night we met."

"When you wonder why I don't lay down for you, it's because of the night we met and all other nights like it. God, I was so easy for you, wasn't I?"

"I was easy for you, too, back then. We were kids, doing what kids do. Remember?"

"I remember all right. I remember the sacrifices I made for you."

"Caleb was a sacrifice for both of us, but I wouldn't change the way things turned out for anything."

"What about for a blowjob?" She turned her chin toward him, a sly smile creeping onto her face. "Would you change it for a blowjob, Luke?"

"Our son for a blowjob? What kind of a question is that?"

"Don't worry. I know you don't have the balls to find the right woman to do it. Just remember what you sacrifice when you think about trying to."

"Do you want me to go? Are you trying to push me away?"

"I don't know."

"Do you understand why I leave?"

"What I don't understand is why you keep coming back."

"Do you want this to work, Diane? Is it ever going to work, or are we killing time?"

"I don't know."

"Well, before we kill each other, do you think we can figure it out?"

"I don't know!"

"What do you want me to do? If I try, you turn your back on me. If

I don't, you're offended. Tell me what to do, and I'll do it."

"I don't know what you should do."

"No, you know I should go to work. You know I should support you and the kids. You know I don't make half the money you wish I did, and you know I shouldn't bother you when I get the urge to love you in the middle of the night. What else do you know? What else should I do?"

A cold stare settled on him. Not a trace of tears was present in her eyes, although he felt like bursting into waterworks.

"I don't know." She rolled onto her back, now studying the ceiling. "There's still water damage, from that leak in the roof last spring."

He leaned over her and kissed her frigid lips, gauging her reaction, putting some effort into it, parting his lips.

No response.

He gathered her boyish nightgown with his fingers and caressed her stomach.

She continued her staring contest with the ceiling.

He worked his way up to her breasts, and bit into her neck.

As if she didn't want to witness his next act, she closed her eyes.

He worked a knee between her legs and bunched the nightgown above her scarce bosom, at her neck. He rolled his tongue over her nipples, covering every inch of her flesh with his mouth, and licked her down to her navel.

Nothing.

Slowly, he pulled off her underpants and nibbled gently on her clitoris. He entered her with his tongue and brushed her softly. She tasted sweet and...pregnant. But that wasn't possible.

She lay there, rigid and motionless.

Still, he worked. There had to be something left in her. There had to be. He pulled her legs up and rested her thighs on his shoulders.

She pulled the nightgown down to hide her breasts.

He continued to eat, growing more aroused by the second, while she lay in boredom. He wrote the alphabet inside her with his tongue. Three times. Slowly. *Come on, Diane.* He hummed onto her, simulating vibration, caressed her up and down, inside and out, his hands and mouth working for a favorable response.

Ready to take her by force, he backed away. There was nothing left in her; he'd been wrong to try to create what had dried up long ago. She avoided looking him in the eye.

"Go ahead," she whispered.

"Touch me first."

Nothing again.

"Is it me?" he asked. "If you pretend you're with someone else, does it feel good? Did any of that feel good?"

She didn't answer.

"I don't want it this way. I want it, I want you, but not like this."

She reached for her underpants.

"Good night, Diane."

CHAPTER 10

A radio sounded outside. Kimberley, dressed in a yellow sundress, raised the kitchen shades and peered outside to see Luke's pickup truck parked in front of the fourth stall door. She quickly picked her jaw up off the floor and opened a window. "Hello."

"'Morning, Mrs. Roderick." Luke squinted into the sunshine, wrinkling his nose. "I don't suppose I can trouble you for a cup of coffee?"

"No, you can't. I already have one man in my life who doesn't have time for me, and you're eight days late."

"So is my wife."

Butterflies kicked up like a tornado in her gut. "Late? As in pregnant?"

"Look, I'm sorry I haven't called. Can I come in?"

Suddenly dizzy, nauseous, and encompassed by a whirlwind of emotion ranging from anger to self-pity, she nodded and turned to unlock the breakfast room door. Luke wasn't supposed to procreate. He was supposed to spend his days with his hand against her baby, flattering her, and trying to hurdle his way into her bed.

Where did he get off impregnating another woman, when she'd relied on him for the attention she couldn't possibly receive from the man she'd married? Brennan hadn't called to say he'd arrived safely at this week's office, or left a message with the number of the hotel, in case of emergency, as his replacement cell phone had yet to arrive. Damn it, she needed more of Luke; she couldn't share him with the three people he was obligated to, let alone with a brand new baby. She sat at the table, forcing her lower lip out of a pout, and dropped her head into her hands.

"You all right?" He carried the scent of fresh-cut grass indoors with him.

She willed away tears. "Fine."

He took the chair opposite her and opened his hand; slowly, her hand crawled to his.

"But Brennan... Oh, never mind."

"What did he do now?"

"Long story."

"I've got time for long stories."

"Not this one." At last, she raised her head. "When's she due?"

"She hasn't told me yet," he said, "but I know her schedule. I pay attention. And yesterday, I found the test in the trash. Positive."

"Congratulations."

The scar at his eye creased with his squint. "You aren't happy for me."

"I should be, I know. It's just..." She took a deep breath and dabbed at her eyes. "It's just horrendously bad timing."

"It's not mine."

She blinked. "Pardon me?"

"The baby."

"How do you know?"

"None of my guys have seen the inside of a uterus since January. Five months, if you're keeping score."

"I'm sorry."

He squeezed her hand. "It happens, you know?"

She nodded. "Unfortunately."

"So are we ever going to let this happen? You and me?"

"I'm pregnant."

"I wish it were my baby."

"Mine or Diane's?"

"Both."

It figured. "Do any of the men in my life know how they feel about me?"

"Give me a reason to walk away."

"I think Diane gave you one."

"Well, give me another." His index finger caressed the top of her hand, and his remaining three rubbed back and forth in her grasp. Back and forth, back and forth.

His fingers moved through hers, sparking a deep-seated urge between her legs. Wow, if he made love with other parts the way he used his hands... She imagined those fingers slowly pressing into her tunnel and dragging out. In, in, in, in. Out, out, out, out.

"I saw you," he whispered. "I came for three nights without seeing you, but then, right on time, at three, I saw you, eating ice cream, crying."

"Did anyone see you?"

"You cry more than you should."

Were her panties damp?

"Tell me, beautiful girl, do you make love to him when he's slobbering drunk?"

She did that night, reaching orgasm with her eyes closed, whispering a name. And the intense feeling between her legs now inspired her to whisper it again: "Luke."

"Do you?" He stared hard at her, his fingers keeping the same, slow rhythm against her hand.

A shudder ran through her, and she licked her lips.

A lascivious grin overtook him. "Whatever I'm doing right, let me know, and I'll keep doing it."

Her cheeks flushed with color and she straightened. "Let's just say you're good at what you do."

"You don't know what I can do."

"I can't know."

"Do you ever think we should just...go with it?"

All the time. Family-shmamily, right?

"Look." He licked his full bottom lip. "I know you try. You're a good wife. You weren't looking for someone to fill Brennan's shoes Sunday night through Friday afternoon when you found me. But this is natural. Two beautiful people who found each other at a time when—"

"Stop, Luke." Her words escaped her in a hushed whisper, although she'd intended them to be severe.

"I know you're not screwing the mailman. I'm different. I'm special when it comes to you." His fingers continued to massage her hand. "Right?"

Special? Like Jason? She nodded. "Yes."

He released her hand and in a split second, disappeared under the table. Before she knew what was happening, he'd rested his head in her lap, his hands working their way against her backside.

God, he felt good. Hands under her dress; fingers wiggling into her panties.

"Don't." She shifted, but her movement only enabled his swift hands to reach their destination faster.

"Relax," he whispered against her thighs. "I promise, Kimber, I'll be good. But I just have to know first." A thick finger wrestled against her clitoris for half a moment before another pushed into her.

"Oh, God!"

His wedding band rubbed against her insides, dragged along her walls and exited. How could something so wrong feel so good?

Again, he pressed into her.

"Please," she whispered, "don't make me want this."

"Do you want it? Do you want me?"

"God, yes. But..."

His hands slid away, and he reappeared in his chair, licking her taste from his fingers.

Why would Diane refuse that kind of pleasure?

"Sorry," he said with a schoolboy grin. "I had to."

She frowned.

He headed toward the door, a hard seven-and-five-eighths bulging at his crotch. "Thanks for the coffee."

She'd yet to pour a mug.

"I should get back to work, beautiful girl."

"About that." Breathing was a struggle.

"Yeah?"

"What do I owe you?"

He smiled. "Another cup of coffee."

* * *

"Let's go for a walk, Mommy," Allison said, jolting her from the same daydream occupying her thoughts all day—of Luke's fingers treating her well. "To the park."

"You're too sleepy, Allie, and I can't carry you when you get too tired to walk."

"I'll ride, Mommy. In my stroller. Please?"

She blinked away thoughts of climaxing under Luke's rugged body. "All right."

"Yippee! I'll change outfits."

"Can't you wear what you're wearing?"

"These are play clothes. Not park clothes."

"Make it quick." Twenty minutes later, she pushed her daughter in the stroller, walking around the block and through Satchel Park, rubbing her engorged clitoris between her pregnant thighs.

More. She needed more. One night wouldn't be enough. A week wouldn't come close. One night a week for the rest of her life. Not fair, not enough, but it would have to suffice. *Oh God, I'm falling in love with him.*

* * *

"Kimmy, Kimmy Coco Bop." She looked up at her house to see Brennan, lolling on the front porch swing, dress shirt unbuttoned and untucked, home hours earlier than she'd expected.

"Brennan. Hi." She swallowed hard, wondering if the scent of sex steamed from her pores. Did she smell like Luke? Did she taste like him? "Where's the repairman? He was staining the new garage door."

"Gone when I got here."

Whew. She bent to unbuckle Allison from the stroller.

"Let me get her, Kimmy. You shouldn't be lifting her when you don't have to."

She ignored her husband, hoisted her daughter, and held her tight to her chest. "I'm going to take a fast shower," she whispered, hurrying inside and up the stairs.

"Wait a minute, Kim."

"I'll be quick, but I'm hot. Nauseous." She deposited Allison onto her princess bed and rushed to the master suite. She yanked off her clothes and pulled on the faucet. Yet seconds before she stepped into the shower, Brennan swooped her into his arms and deposited her naked body onto the dressing table.

"Bren, I'm sweating."

"Good. Let me sweat with you." His hands grazed along the contours of her breasts, and he dropped to his knees, darting his tongue into her slick, stimulated opening.

Her thighs tightened at his cheeks, and she closed her eyes, quivering. Coming. Gushing on his tongue.

* * *

"Do you have something to tell me?" Luke asked, tossing a shop towel over a puddle of urine next to the back door.

Diane crossed her arms under her breasts. "One more accident on my floor, and that dog's getting the needle, Luke."

"I don't mean about Derby. About you."

She took a deep breath. "I'm going to my sister's tonight. I think we could both use a break."

He nodded. "Sure."

"I'll leave the children, if you think you can handle them in morning. I'll be back before your session with Dr. Schaeffer."

"Yeah, I don't think I'm going to go to counseling anymore."

"Suit yourself." She turned toward the stairs.

"Anything else you want to tell me?"

She shook her head. "Not especially."

* * *

The worst dinner cruise to date. And she'd thought last year's tragedy was insurmountable. Brennan stepped on Kimberley's toes for the eighteenth time. The brisk wind on Lake Michigan made for choppy water and a rocking vessel, and coupled with his drink of choice, his usual suave dance moves were anything but.

"Let's sit down," she said.

"No." He pulled her against his shirt, damp with sweat, and exhaled an atrocious breath in her face.

"I'm tired, Bren."

"What a surprise."

"I'm pregnant."

"So is Gina, and so is Christine. And they're awake."

"I will be, too, by the third trimester."

"Yeah, yeah."

"Brennan, this baby is a choice we made together. I'm sorry it inconveniences you."

"If I ever gave you the impression now was the right time to expand our family, Kimmy..." He shook his head. "You wanted it, you got it. Deal with it."

"We wanted it. Not me. We."

"What's your problem tonight?"

Perhaps the-shot-of-Jack-per-basket during his morning basketball league shouldn't bother her. Maybe the scent of whiskey on his breath, the beads of sweat dripping from his brow, and the slurring since two in the afternoon shouldn't faze her in the least. And, yes, maybe she should even overlook his contempt for this pregnancy. "Nothing, Brennan. I'm having a great time."

"Oh," he whispered into her ear. "Well, I beg your fucking pardon,

Kimmy, but if you're having such a great time—"

"I'm fine, Brennan. Let's just—"

His grip on her hand tightened, and he squeezed her uncomfortably close, against his moist skin. "Maybe you should have a drink. Loosen up. One glass of red wine won't kill the baby, you know."

"I'd rather not."

"Would you rather I throw you into the dinghy and let you paddle back to shore?"

She stepped back, alarmed by his hateful glare, the pure evil seeping through his expression.

"Have a good time," he said. "That's all I ask. Or at least pretend to enjoy yourself. But you won't. Jesus Christ, Kimmy, this night isn't exactly a fucking riot for me either. Do you think I wanted to wear this tie?"

"If the blue tie were so important, you should've gone to the cleaners yourself."

"I work hard. You spend my money." He gripped her wrists, holding her prisoner. "Picking up the dry cleaning isn't brain surgery, and it's the least you can do."

She pulled to free herself, her wrists aching, and immediately looked away when she caught sight of Lauren. The last thing she needed was another pity party, but her best friend had already reached for her. Finally free, Kimberley darted to the ladies' room, rubbing her red wrists, with Lauren at her heels.

"Honey, what happened?" Lauren sat next to Kimberley on a bench.

"I said yes." Tremendous tears soaked her cheeks. "And I regret saying yes every Saturday night. It's no wonder I still reserve a place in my heart for Jason. If this were your life, wouldn't you wish you'd chosen option number one?"

"Kimmy."

"Of the two men who've loved me, why did I say yes to Brennan Roderick?"

"Don't say that. He's a good man, he's just—"

"I don't know what else to say. I mean, why didn't you accept when he proposed to you? What makes you so smart?"

"Honey, what do you want me to do?"

"Push rewind. Please, just push rewind."

"I'll go talk to him."

"It won't make a difference. What's done is done, and you can't erase this constant humiliation, the irreversible hurt. Every goddamn year, every special occasion."

"I'll calm him down. Wait for me here?"

"I assure you, Lauren, I'll be here for the rest of the night. I'm not going back out there."

"Can I get you anything?" Lauren walked toward the door.

"You mean, besides a new husband?"

"Oh, honey." Lauren's pink lips flattened into a line, and she opened the door. "You know he loves you."

Once alone, Kimberley pulled her cell phone from her purse, dialed, and left a message. "Hi. I know it's late, and I can't talk, so don't call me back. But meet me tomorrow. One o'clock. Rain or shine."

* * *

As luck had it, the sun shone.

"Did I ever tell you about the most flattering moment of my life?" Kimberley asked, lying on her stomach in the forest preserve, kicking her feet like a carefree teenager. Luke had been waiting, bearing gifts in the form of a strawberry milkshake and French fries, when she arrived.

With a smile, he mocked her, kicking his feet, too. His lips encircled a red-and-white striped straw, and he sipped from the paper tumbler she held securely against the ground.

"Most flattering moment." His nose wrinkled as he contemplated. "No, Kimber, I haven't heard this one."

For a few moments, she imagined life with him. Waking up with him, kissing him at the door as he left for work in the morning, serving him dinner every night. Being a stepmother to his children, his being Allison's stepfather, her everyday father figure.

Easy. Relaxing. Frightening.

"Well?" He chuckled. "Now that I'm curious…"

"Oh." She blinked away thoughts of forever. "It's nothing, really, just a tiny piece of history that's stayed with me since my sixteenth birthday. When I met his grandmother, Jason held my hand."

"That's it? Anyone could do that."

"His grandmother used to wear a charm bracelet with a commemorative charm for each grandchild, and—"

"What was Jason's charm?"

"A baseball hat, and she was very proud of it, too. She'd show her bracelet to waitresses, doctors, anyone who'd look. Even strangers on the street. And she'd explain each and every charm and why it signified a specific grandchild. And when I met her, Jason gave her a golden four-leaf clover. He said he felt lucky around me."

Luke took hold of her hand, his fingers warm against hers. "Don't worry, Kimberley. I'll hold your hand when you meet my grandmother, too. I promise."

She smiled. "What are you doing next Wednesday?"

"Are you asking me for a date?"

"Of sorts."

* * *

That Wednesday, with her shirt gathered just under her bra, and her jeans unfastened, Kimberly smiled up at Luke. "Were you with Diane the first time she heard your kids' heartbeats?"

"Caleb's. Not Rachael's." He gave her hand a little squeeze, but quickly backed away, keeping one eye on the door. "But I wish I had been. Was Brennan there for Allie's?"

"He had a meeting."

"Hello." Dr. Janus entered the room, fixing his stare on Kimberley's file. "How are we today?"

Although her obstetrician hadn't given Luke a second glance, she cleared her throat and delivered the fib she'd practiced all the way to the doctor's office. "My husband is out of town, so I brought a proxy. This is my brother."

The doctor glanced at Luke over a file and only mumbled a noncommittal hello, but when he turned to Kimberley, a small smile touched his lips. "You're getting a little baby bubble down here."

"It's ice cream," she said.

"You're only up three pounds, but you'll want to watch that ice cream from now on, Kim, all right? Now let's see if we can find this heartbeat."

"Eat if you're hungry," Luke interjected.

The cold Doppler met her skin.

"Are you going to find out if it's a boy or girl?"

The doctor probed around her abdomen.

"No, I like to be surprised."

"Diane has to know. It drives her crazy until she knows."

The doctor adjusted the Doppler and glanced at the chart. "You're ten weeks?"

"Almost eleven."

"We knew with Caleb, just had a feeling. And the ultrasound proved us right. Rachael...well, I've never been in tune with her but—"

"Ten weeks? Ten-and-a-half?" The doctor piped up.

"Yes."

"I can't find it." The doctor removed the device and wiped gel from Kimberley's skin.

"What?" Instantly, tears filled her eyes. "What does that mean?"

Luke crouched at her side.

"It doesn't necessarily mean anything, Kim," the doctor said. "It just means that—"

"Try again," Luke said. His brown eyes darted to the doctor's gaze, but swiftly returned to hers.

"I don't think I'm going to hear it today, but we can try next week. Sometimes I can't pick it up until week fifteen."

"Please," Luke said.

The doctor shook his head. "I won't hear it. Could be too early."

"But I'm almost eleven weeks." She sniffled. "We heard Allie's at nine."

Luke grasped her hand. "Can we have a few minutes?"

"Of course."

Once alone with Luke, she allowed tears to flow like mad waterfalls and covered her eyes. "You're a God-fearing man. Is this my due penance for my repeated wrongs? For aborting Jason's child? For cheating on my husband?"

"Look at me. Kimber, look at me."

She struggled to lock her gaze on him.

"Breathe."

She shook her head.

"Breathe, Kimber."

Their entwined hands pressed relentlessly against her uterus, and his other hand tangled into her hair.

"It's because of the abortion. That's what he'll say."

"What who'll say? Brennan?"

"He'll say it's because of the abortion."

"You heard the doctor."

"Something's wrong. I'm not a moron, Luke. I know we should've heard it, and I know why we didn't."

"Look at me."

And this time, when their eyes met, softness overcame her. Amid the chaos of the moment, a sense of calm settled in the air between them, hanging in his gaze. She exhaled, inhaled, and exhaled again, breathing in time with Luke.

"That's my girl. In and out, in and out."

She released his hand and wiped away tears.

"Until you know for sure, there's nothing wrong," he said. "A woman in your condition can't afford the stress of worry." His hands moved to her open jeans, and he refastened them. Seemingly accidentally, his fingers caressed the sides of her breasts as he gingerly pulled her shirt down over her stomach. "Don't tell your husband if you think he'll blame you. We'll come back next week."

She nodded, stifling the last of her tears and pulling him close. "I'll bet you were one hell of a labor coach."

A dry kiss landed upon her cheek. "You're right."

* * *

Kimberley didn't know if she was going to tell Brennan about the baby's heartbeat until she saw him Friday afternoon, when disgust made the decision for her. He didn't deserve to know.

"Hey there, angel pie." With glazed and unfocused eyes, Brennan meandered across the great room, toward Allison, who abandoned her toys the moment she saw him.

"Daddy!" She scrambled to her feet and began to run.

Yet before she reached her father, Kimberley held her tight. "You can hug Daddy later." She swung her around, depositing her body between her daughter and Brennan.

"I want to hug him now." Allison pouted.

"I wanna hug you, too, angel pie."

She glared at her husband over her shoulder.

"What? I'm fine." He grinned. "A whole lot richer, too."

"Mommy?" Allison twisted Kimberley's wedding ring. "Why can't I say hi to Daddy?"

Her heart sank, and she released her daughter, who shot to Brennan's side and climbed into his arms. He tossed her into the air and covered her cheeks with kisses.

"Down, Daddy. Let's play."

Brennan put her down and staggered around the room while Allison chased him, laughing and oblivious to her father's condition—and to Kimberley's.

Baby bubble. More likely, she was just fat.

"Allie, calm down," Kimberley said. "You'll get hurt."

The child ignored the warning, screeching as she reached out to touch her father. "Tag, Daddy. You're It."

"Brennan, please."

He grabbed Allison and again tossed her into the air. "A flying angel pie. There she goes again. Way up high." It would have been endearing, had her husband been sober.

Kimberley couldn't watch and wait for an accident. She slipped into the kitchen and opened the phone directory. With a yellow marker, she highlighted three-quarters of a column and tossed the book onto her husband's desk, page exposed: Addictions Counseling.

"I don't know what else to do," she muttered.

Out of the corner of her eye, she spotted a pink slip of paper sticking out of a desk drawer. She pulled out an over-drawn notice from the bank, dated a week ago. She sighed and shoved it back into the drawer before leaving the room.

"All right, Allie," she called down the hall. "Bed time."

* * *

"I love you." Kimberley stared out at the sun rising over the ninth green.

Brennan cuddled behind her, his arm slinked around her, and his hand softly squeezing her right breast.

"I love you, too," he whispered, his hung over, whiskey breath hot on the back of her neck.

"But if you ever come home in that condition again, and insist on playing with our daughter, I'm leaving you."

"I'm sorry." He tightened his arm around her.

"I don't care anymore, Brennan, how sorry you are. She's little, she doesn't understand, and she doesn't deserve this."

"What do you want me to say?"

"Nothing, Bren. You're a father. Act like one."

Silent for a few minutes, he cleared his throat. "I love you, Coco Bop."

"I love you, too, but you need help, and you need to get it now."

"I'm fine. I'm handling things."

"Are you handling the finances, too? I found the over-drawn slip from the bank."

"Misunderstanding."

"Was it?"

"Actually, Allie's ballet tuition is what put us over. You don't record debits in the register, Kim."

"Yes, I do. I was managing a checkbook when I was in junior high, for God's sake."

"Anyway, we have upward around fifty grand in the savings. I just forgot to transfer." His hand trailed down to her abdomen. "Do you think it's a boy or a girl?"

Maybe neither. "Brennan, do you want this baby?"

"What, I had a couple drinks on the plane yesterday, spent a few hours at a card table, and suddenly I don't want this baby?"

"I didn't mean it like that."

"Say what you mean because I work too damn hard to deal with this guilt trip every Saturday morning." He sprang from the bed, making a beeline to the bathroom.

She heard the unzipping of his travel shaving case, the rattling of his aspirin bottle, and the gushing of the faucet.

"I'm just tired," she said, when he returned. "And I've got a lot on my mind."

He sat on the mattress, his back to her. "Yeah, I know. Manicures and ballet lessons really take it all out of you."

"Your job ends when you walk in that door. I've been on the clock since the second she was born, and don't you dare tell me what I do is easy."

"God, you're out of control when you're pregnant. I understand the hormones, and the weight gain, and the nausea, but tell me it'll end before this pregnancy does."

"It may be over now," she said, crawling from the bed and whipping a pillow at him. Quickly, and crying all the while, she brushed her teeth and pulled her hair into a scraggly ponytail. She squeezed her maybe-pregnant thighs and breasts into a stretchy, casual dress and waved on her way out of the house.

She should have told him about not hearing the baby's heartbeat, but then he'd wonder why she waited to tell him, why she'd answered with a simple "Fine," when he'd asked how the appointment had gone. And then, she'd have to explain Luke.

Luke. She fished her cell phone from among tissues, Happy Meal toys, even a pair of Allison's tap shoes, from her purse, and punched memory 8. "Can you meet me?"

"What's wrong?"

"Nothing. I need to see you."

"The club?"

"Forest preserve. Our place."

"Ten minutes?"

"See you." She clicked off the phone and immediately dialed Lauren. "I don't want you to think I've left him yet, but I need some time. I promise I'm going back home."

Lauren yawned. "Honey, what happened?"

"We couldn't find the heartbeat."

"Oh, Kim."

"And I don't want to worry Brennan, so I haven't told him yet, but I'm...I'm just not myself, so I need to get away."

"All right."

"Would you mind... Could you keep Brennan company? Tell him I'll be back before lunch? And tell him I love him?"

"Sure."

"Thanks. I owe you."

Good thing she'd gone to law school. Where else would she have learned to manipulate words and evoke favorable responses? Lauren hadn't guessed Kimberley was using her to keep Brennan cornered. He'd looked for her last time; without Lauren's insistence, perhaps he'd look again.

And he wouldn't like what he saw, if he happened to find her.

* * *

Usually, even amid a workout, Kimberley looked perfectly put together. This morning, however, she appeared more natural. Unruly. No lipstick, hair sprouting from a hair tie like a weeping willow in the wind. He didn't think it possible that a woman could be more attractive than she on a normal day, but... *Wow.* Luke sat on the dirt next to her, brushing a kiss upon her cheek. "Hi, beautiful girl."

"It isn't the baby," she whispered, grasping his hand. "I still don't know..."

"So what happened?"

"I don't want to talk. Not today."

He nodded, caressing her knuckles with his thumb, stumbling over the mountainous diamond in her wedding band. "Are you all right?"

"If things were all right, do you think I'd be here?" A fire raged in her eyes. Anger. Passion. Sorrow.

He wiggled her ring. She curled her finger, as if to curb his determination, but when he raised his glance to hers, she relaxed. He removed the ring and dropped it into her purse. Slowly, he leaned to her, cupping her face in his left hand.

"Take yours off, too," she whispered.

With little difficulty, he slipped his ring over his knuckle and it followed suit, into her purse.

"Are you going to put it back on?" she asked.

What a question. "Yeah." He leaned to her again, holding her cheek in the contour of his hand, tracing her soft lower lip with his thumb. He'd waited too long for this moment, had to make it perfect. Slow, so he'd remember it, in case it didn't happen again.

He licked his lips, and she sighed a seductive groan.

"Kimber."

Her eyelashes flickered open, and she parted her lips to respond. He rippled his tongue into her mouth like sperm into an egg. Tenderly, provocatively, he bit into her mouth. She tasted of cinnamon toothpaste, smelled like Ivory soap.

His arms flexed around her. His hands roamed over her firm but feminine backside, against her large breasts, beneath her dress and along her inner thighs. He dragged a finger against her clitoris, just to gauge her reaction.

A sharp intake of air and a sweet, "Ohhh."

"I need you, Kimber." He pulled her across his lap so she straddled him. "I need you," he whispered against her lips. "My God, I need you."

Her heart beat against him like pulsating club music. "This is crazy." Her lips brushed against his when she spoke. "But I want you, too. All of you."

"Are you ready to walk away from all that?" His thumb traced a nipple, feeling it harden with his touch. "I can't give you that house, that ring…"

"Is that what you think I want?" She pressed her hips to his pelvis, and he solidified to his full seven-and-five-eighths. Suddenly, her hands were at his fly, popping the button on his jeans. She slipped her hand inside, raking her fingers against his erection.

"Oh, beautiful girl."

"I don't want the house, that ring. None of that's me."

He trailed his thumb over her lips. "Tell me what you want."

"I want…" Her stare was serious and mesmerizing.

"Please," he whispered, lowering his mouth to a breast, laving her through her clothing. He subtly ground up against her in a simulation of sex.

"Do you have anything?" Her fingers laced through his hair.

"Like what?"

"A condom."

Protection. Of course. If he'd had any idea *this* was what she'd had in mind, he would have brought condoms by the truckload. "I'm healthy. And you're already pregnant." He maneuvered her panties aside and pressed in a finger. So hot. So wet. And as he already knew, so deep.

He lifted her against his cock, shuddering with the feel of a responsive, wet woman aligned with his erection. "Tell me what you want."

"You're not naïve." She moved against him, her lips on his neck.

"I'm not going to do it unless you tell me."

"Do it," she breathed, wiggling to bring her opening in line with him, rocking over him, working his tip inside. "God, you feel good."

He pressed upward with more force, and in two plunges, he'd buried himself. "Too good to be wrong." He squeezed her hips, slammed his pelvis into hers. He refused to break their visual connection, and her eyes seemed a greener shade of shamrock amid passion.

The rustling of leaves in the distance drew her attention, but he caught her by the chin and turned her face back to his.

"Someone's coming," she whispered.

"That better be you." And he kissed her, slow and passionate, seven-and-five-eighths penetrating in thorough strokes, her clit meticulously rubbing against his abdomen. And if it felt that good for him...

The snap of a twig jolted her, and she tensed. "Luke—"

He devoured her mouth, swallowing her words, and he drove home with each grind of his hips, filling her, pleasing her. One hand gingerly crushed a breast, the other flicked against her clit, enticing her to shiver.

Voices from the path grew louder.

"Kimber..." Sweat broke at his brow, on his chest. His balls hardened, ready to erupt. *There it is.*

"Someone's—"

In a swift motion, he lifted her from his seven-and-five eighths, and gently placed her on the ground next to him. Semen, still spouting, dripped down the length of him. Damn it, an additional two seconds and he could have shot every ounce of his fluid into her. He tucked his rigid penis into his jeans.

With wide eyes, she touched her swollen lips.

A family of four walked past, smiling their good-mornings, oblivious to the adulterous events that had just transpired.

"You didn't get there," he said, running his hands through his hair. "I wanted you to get there."

She blinked. "I should go."

"I want to see you again."

"Give me a call." She reached for her purse, wiped a tear from her eye.

"Aw, don't do that, beautiful girl." He touched her on the chin. "Don't regret this. Please."

"No, I'm fine. Just...call me, all right?"

Her rear end swayed when she walked away.

CHAPTER 11

Luke seeped out of her vagina, a constant blinking light in her mind: she'd had sex—unprotected—with another man, crossed a line she couldn't erase. And worse, he was everything she'd imagined him to be. She'd never forget it, and she didn't want to.

At the gym, she washed the scent of sex from her body, using the complimentary shampoo in the club shower stall, drying with an abrasive, club-issued towel.

She stared into the mirror, combing through her frizzy hair with her fingers. *Adulteress.* But was it wrong to pursue a better life for herself? For her children?

Marriages ended all the time—her once-career stood testament to that—and it wasn't as if she hadn't tried. On the contrary, she'd tried too hard, considering the effort had been one-sided.

After nearly eight years, she hadn't helped Brennan by staying, constantly forgiving him. Perhaps Brennan, too, would be better off without the tethers of marriage binding him.

What would Jason think of her cheating on her husband, leaving Brennan for a man she'd known for only a few weeks? Would he be disappointed in her? Would he even care?

She glanced at her left hand, panicking for a split second at the absence of her wedding ring. But why would it be there, when Luke had taken it off? She rummaged through her purse, slipped it on, and searched for Luke's. How could she have forgotten to give it back to him?

She emptied her purse, setting Allison's tap shoes atop the counter with a *clink, clink*, tossing random receipts and ratty-looking, but unused, tissues into the trash. Her hand smoothed against the bottom of her shoulder bag, but Luke's ring wasn't there. Maybe she'd given it back to him after all.

In a daze, she left the club and drove toward home, reluctant to arrive.

She stopped at the Jasmine Vine for a cup of decaffeinated raspberry.

She purchased two-for-one bath salts at Lyndi's as a thank you and apology to Lauren, who'd fielded more than a few tirades lately.

And she stopped at the drycleaner.

"Oh, hello, 3-4-3-7."

"Hi."

"I have no clothes, 3-4-3-7. You pick up Wednesday, no?"

"Did I?"

"Oh, pregnant lady always forget."

"I'm sorry. Are you sure?"

"I sure. Don't worry. See you Wednesday."

* * *

Shit. In the cab of his truck, parked in front of Sugar Plum Dance Studio, Luke briskly rubbed his hands over his face, washing it with air. Good sex for him, but hardly a show of his best work. He'd finished too quickly, let Kimber walk away, and judging by her pouting exit, he'd probably never see her again. And double shit, she still had his wedding ring.

He took a deep breath and dialed her cell for the fourth time. Again, no answer. He fisted his left hand, which felt naked without the ring he'd worn for the past eight years, through Diane's adultery, the birth of two babies, even through separations. But things were different now. He'd made love to Kimberley Roderick. This time, he'd chosen to stray.

"God, I hope she's worth it," he muttered. But would he ever see her again? He lifted his head from his hands, and the banner in the storefront window caught his eye: Spring Recital. Of course.

He made his way into the studio, still sticky at the crotch from ejaculation. "One ticket to Saturday's show, please," he said to a young woman behind the counter.

The pretty blonde, aged about twenty and wearing a leotard, smiled from behind the counter. "You don't look familiar. Do you have a child in the show?"

"No, just a...a friend. Diane's never introduced my girl to activities like this."

Dr. Schaeffer's probable commentary sounded in his head: *Have you ever tried to introduce your daughter to dance? Why is Diane wrong for not trying, but you're always in the clear?*

"Here's a fall schedule of classes, if you're interested."

He took the offered pink flyer. "You know what? Why don't you make that two tickets? I'll bring my daughter with me. She might enjoy the show." Maybe she'd start dance classes in the fall. Maybe then, Diane would realize he was a good father, interested in his children's lives. Even though not a cell of his DNA existed in Rachael's tiny body, he loved her as if she were his own. And damn it, he wanted her to experience the world.

* * *

When Kimberley returned home, Brennan and Lauren sat on the screened porch, sharing a breakfast of fruit and toast, unaware of her arrival, as she'd parked way down the drive, behind Lauren's car. The genuine, silent chemistry between them amazed her. They'd probably been flawless in bed together, too.

Had they ever considered rolling in the hay once more?

Take him, Lauren. Take him off my hands.

Ten feet away, Allison frolicked in the sandbox with Pink.

"Hi, baby," Kimberley whispered.

Allison raised her head and broke into a sprint, screeching, "Mommy!"

Simultaneously, Brennan and Lauren looked up from their breakfast. "Hi, Kimmy." Lauren dabbed the corners of her mouth with a cloth napkin. "I hope her dress is all right. I didn't know if she should be playing in the sand, but she's choosey about clothes and—"

"It's fine," Kimberley said, opening her arms to Allison. So Brennan had allowed his ex-girlfriend to dress their daughter. He'd already replaced his wife, if only for the morning.

"I missed you, Mommy." Allison spun her wedding ring.

"I missed you, too, Allie."

She fingered her mother's nail polish. "Pretty color. What's it called?"

"Bordeaux." She glanced up at Brennan, who managed a smile. On the table in front of him, amidst his breakfast dishes, sat the telephone book she'd highlighted last night, closed.

* * *

"I want to take Rachael to a ballet recital," Luke said, sitting on his side of the bed. He unbuttoned his flannel shirt, a fading scent of Kimberley emanating from its threads.

"Why?" Diane puttered around the dresser, opening and slamming drawers.

"I thought it might be good for her. For us, I mean, to spend some time together. Daddy to daughter."

"She won't want to go with you."

"Why not?"

She slammed another drawer. "Because taking her to some ridiculous recital once doesn't make you Father of the Year. She realizes you favor Caleb. God, she'd have to be brain-dead not to see it."

"I don't—"

"Where is it?" The dresser shook with the slamming of the last drawer.

"What are you looking for?"

"Your wedding ring."

"You're looking for my ring?" He cleared his throat, his heart picking up pace. "Why?"

"I left for one day, and you're not wearing it anymore."

"Aw, Diane, don't read into it. I sprained my finger at the gym this morning."

"How very convenient."

He stared at his hands. "Talk about convenient. I found the test."

Her skin went wan. "Test?"

"In the trash. A positive pregnancy test."

She shook her head. "I don't know what you're talking about."

"I didn't imagine it, Diane. I saw it. A generic, over-the-counter pregnancy test with a positive result."

She slumped into bed, her back to him, and reached for her book.

"Where did you go last night? To tell this guy—is it Radcliffe again?—you're knocked up?"

"Keep your voice down."

"Answer my question."

"I told you yesterday. I spent the night with my sister. Call her if you'd like."

He crashed into his pillow, exhausted. No need to probe her with questions she obviously wouldn't answer, and no need pry her legs apart tonight either. Fourteen hours ago, he'd made love to a passionate angel. He'd finished inside her, such an intimate occurrence.

A nice thought to fall asleep to, to dream about.

Around three in the morning, he awoke with an intense erection. Not bothering to leave the bed, he reached down and rubbed it out, leaving a puddle just south of his wife's derriere.

* * *

Kimberley stared at her ringing cell phone. A battle of will ensued between her heart and her head, but in the end, her heart claimed victory. "Hello."

"Hey, beautiful girl."

Silent for a few seconds, lulled by the tenor of his voice, she knew she'd done the right thing in answering the call. "What can I do for you?"

"Where should I start?"

She smiled at the sound of his laughter. "I'm sorry I haven't called, but—"

"No need to explain. I'll see you at three."

"I don't think we should see each other right now."

"If you think I'm letting you go back there alone, you're crazy."

Back there? "Oh, the doctor."

"What did you think I meant?"

"My appointment's at four."

"I know. I made it for you, remember? Can you meet me at three? Just to talk?"

Against her better judgment, she said, "I'll call Lauren and see if she can take Allie an hour earlier."

"Good. How are you feeling otherwise?"

"Fine."

"Any morning sickness?"

"Not in the past ten days."

"That doesn't mean anything. I'll be waiting at your doctor's office at three, unless I hear from you."

She climbed into Luke's truck at three-fifteen, and because a large, cuddly-looking dog consumed the better portion of the floor, she propped her feet on the dashboard.

"Hey." His hand glided to her lap and rested on her thigh. "Thanks for coming."

She looked to a snapshot on his dashboard. "Is this Caleb? And Diane?" The child had Luke's eyes, and the woman's hair was the color of corn silk.

"Yeah. Caleb's second birthday." He squeezed her thigh. "About the other day...I can't stop thinking about it."

"Try." Finally, her gaze trailed from the photograph and met his.

"Are you still thinking about it?"

She began to shake her head, but then nodded. "It hasn't left my mind."

"I'm not living in a dream world. I know I have to share it with your husband, but I can't forget your passion."

She took his hand. "What do you think will happen if we don't hear the heartbeat today?"

He licked his lips and took a deep breath. "The doctor will probably want to take a look to see for sure, but—"

"But you think I'll probably miscarry."

"No matter what happens, I won't let you think it's your fault. I won't let him blame you." His thumb brushed over her fingers.

She rested her head against his shoulder, and suddenly, he was Jason. Outside the abortion clinic, the beat of Jason's heart, the rising and falling of his chest had reminded her of his mortality. Had reminded her of what she'd taken from an innocent baby.

* * *

"I want hordes of children." Luke's eyes scanned the walls of the examination room. "Five or six maybe."

She unbuttoned her shorts and lay on the examination table. "You'd better have a harem. Very few women can endure pregnancy five or six times." She gathered her shirt up under her bra, exposing her stomach.

"You know, I think a lot of families live with the husband thinking he's the father of the children when he isn't."

"I spent a year in the courtroom, litigating filings of divorce, due to undeniable adultery, proven with the birth of a child."

"My father didn't stick around, and we were his." Luke shook his head. "Rachael isn't mine, but when it all came down to it, I wanted Diane and me to last forever, so what choice did I have? But when there's someone like you out there, when you need me... I can't pass off another one. I won't."

"Do you really know she isn't yours?"

His left hand landed upon her stomach. "It doesn't matter. I love her anyway."

"You're a good father."

"I'm going to get you pregnant. Probably in the first few months after you have this baby. If you want me to step in and take care of you, I will, but if you'd rather let Brennan assume responsibility, I won't interfere."

"Don't say things like—"

The doctor walked in.

If the doctor noticed the location of Luke's hand—inappropriate, considering he was supposed to be her brother—he didn't comment or blink an eye. Luke slowly removed his hand from her body.

God, he isn't wearing his wedding ring.

"Let's see," the doctor said, perusing her chart. "Almost twelve weeks. Maybe this little one will talk to us today."

She grasped Luke's naked hand. *Please, let me hear it.*

Together, they listened for the comforting *whoosh, whoosh, whoosh* of a fetus' heartbeat, but the Doppler registered only static, fuzz, and the occasional gastrointestinal gurgle.

"Well," the doctor said, removing the device. "Any bleeding?"

She focused on Luke's eyes, which drooped like a sad puppy's. "None."

"That's a good sign. Let's schedule an ultrasound. If we can't hear it, maybe we'll be able to see it."

Halfway through the parking lot, Luke's voice pierced the dead air. "Will you say something?" He opened the passenger side door of his truck, and in she climbed, next to the massive Golden Retriever filling much of the bench.

"You aren't wearing your wedding ring."

His brow furrowed, and he nimbly climbed up next to her and closed the door. "Are you okay?"

"What's 'okay'? If this baby is gone, there's nothing I can do to bring it back."

"Don't think like that. The doctor said no bleeding was a good sign."

"How old are you?"

He cracked a smile. "How old are you?"

"Twenty-nine."

"I'll be thirty-two next month."

"Did you ever think, growing up, that your life would be such a mess?"

A sigh escaped him. "Are you all right?"

"Not really." She shook her head. "How do you feel about me?"

"I...I want to know what your favorite kind of ice cream is because I eat ice cream every day, too. Sometimes twice."

"What?"

"I want to know your maiden name, whether you considered keeping it. I want to know if you breastfed Allison, whether you regret your decision, either way. How many pairs of panties are stashed in your lingerie drawer? Pairs you want to wear, but don't have an occasion for. Pairs you wear when you want to veg out in front of the television. Pairs you wear when you want to turn someone on. And last, but not at all least, I want to know what Jason did to captivate you because, as far as I see it, no man on this earth deserves you, least of all a man who left you."

Her jaw dropped.

His eyebrows darted upward in expectation. "Well?"

"I can't explain Jason and me. I never could."

"I'm jealous of Jason. And if I'm jealous of anyone, I should be jealous of the man with the liberty to make love to you, day in and day out, but I don't feel threatened by your husband because I don't feel like you love him."

"You're wrong."

"Am I?"

"I resent his addictions. Allison and I stand in line behind his job, his gambling, his drinking, and his friends, and I have no leverage when it comes to anything financial. Our money is his money, and he won't let me earn my own. But he's my husband. I love him."

"In that case"—Luke massaged his bare wedding ring finger—"you should get back to him."

CHAPTER 12

In the dim light of her kitchen in late evening, Kimberley faced her laptop screen, staring at Jason's street address, phone number, and e-mail address, usually unlisted. Yes, he'd bought his parents' house, and if that were any indication, his dreams were becoming reality. Quickly, as if the information would disappear, she jotted down the information and glanced at the clock.

Nine-thirty. Far too late to call, should he have small children. And if he'd yet to procreate, he'd probably be holding the hourglass tightly around that tiny, silk-clad waist, watching old movies until they drifted off to dreamland.

Perhaps an e-mail would be better. She typed, "jldevon—" But no. That "jl" could stand for Jason and Linda. Besides, what would she say? E-mailing didn't seem the way to go either.

She'd waited years to contact him. Perhaps a night to sleep on the proper method would help. She exited the web page, shut down the computer, and tucked the scrap of paper into the hollandaise page of the *Fabulous Gourmet*. Simply having his address would have to suffice for tonight.

She heard a tap on the window and looked up to see Luke, wearing a loose, denim shirt and a straight expression, standing in her screened porch. "Hi."

She glided to the door and met him on the porch.

"I had to see you," he said.

"You shouldn't—"

He kissed her full on the mouth, his tongue flirting with hers, surging her blood to a boiling point. His hands trailed from her backside to her breasts, gingerly caressing her over her pajamas.

She stroked the fingers on his left hand. Still no wedding band.

When he pulled his lips off hers, a low hum filtered through his next breath. "I've missed you, Kimber." He began to lower her to the wicker tabletop.

"It won't hold," she whispered.

"Sure it will." He kissed her again, his fingers grazing against her abdomen, expertly untying the drawstring of her cotton pajama pants. "You're smaller than you think you are."

A shiver ran up her spine when he tucked a hand against her satin panties, rubbing her between her folds of skin, front to back, to front again, rolling her clit between his fingers. He lowered his mouth to a breast, tonguing her, his saliva bleeding through the cotton garment, tantalizing her tender nipple.

"God, I love these breasts." He slipped a hand between the buttons on her shirt, cupping a full, naked breast. "You're killing me."

Inside, the phone rang. She pressed against his chest. "I have to get that."

"No, you don't." He leaned over her again, impeding her trek to the telephone.

"Yes, I do. It'll wake Allie." She escaped his hold, his hands pulling out of her clothing, as if she'd rolled away in bed. "I'm sorry, but I have to." She flung the door open and grabbed the phone. "Hello. Hi, Bren. How was your day?"

Luke followed in silence as she paced the kitchen floor, phone at her ear, and he leaned her back against the island.

He tickled her down her sides, crouching before her and inching her pants over her hips. He slipped the diamond ring off her finger. His lips landed upon her stomach and made their way to her panties. The heat of his breath against her privates, more intense than fire, drew a long gasp from her lips. His tongue flattened against her clitoris, the satin of her panties now dampened by his wet mouth.

She shivered, staring into his eyes, captivated.

"Are you all right, Coco Bop?" Her husband's voice sounded through the receiver.

She gave her head a slight shake. "Don't," she whispered.

"I have to," Luke mouthed against her plump, pregnant thighs.

"Kimmy?" Brennan asked.

Luke whisked off her panties.

She traced the scar near Luke's eye. "Yes."

"Are you listening to me?" Brennan asked.

"Yes."

Luke's pink tongue wiggled into her, brushing her inside and out, slowly, sweetly, his full lips working magic, massaging her flesh.

"Kimmy? Are you there? I asked if we were free to go to Lauren's on the fifteenth."

"Um, Brennan, I have to go."

"Are you all right?"

"Fine. Just…you know."

About to come.

"Pregnant," Brennan said.

Thankfully, she had sense enough not to correct him.

Luke's tongue slowly licked her up and down, lulling her, convincing her to relax. She propped a thigh onto his shoulder, and gyrated against his mouth.

"Uh-huh. Bye, Brennan. Good night."

"I love you."

"I love you, too."

Luke's arms tightened around her, his hands gripping her ass.

She hung up the phone, and haphazardly dropped it to the floor. "Luke, we can't… can't keep—"

"We can," he said against her, licking a long, slow path around the opening of her channel, swirling his tongue over the hard nub her clitoris had become, closing his lips around it and sucking, humming, shoving a thumb into her cunt. "Beautiful girl." He tugged on her shirt and caught her when she dropped to the kitchen floor.

"Tell me what you want," he whispered.

Their lips united in a sugary sweet kiss, and her head spun, the line between right and wrong, cloudy and hazy, his naked seven-and-five-eighths hard against her.

"Oh, God."

He pushed his way inside her. "Beautiful girl."

"We can't."

His steamy gaze pierced into hers, and he slowly rocked further into her body, kissing her deeply.

Her every nerve jittered, and her arms encircled him, squeezing. She tightened against his cock, ready to explode over the entire length of him. An orgasm rumbled deep inside, in response to his stroking her just so perfectly.

"Kiss me," she breathed.

He nipped at her mouth, his tongue dragging along hers.

Her eyes watered, her legs quivered.

"Come on, beautiful," he whispered against her lips.

Every muscle in her body clenched, and at once, she felt a warm gush, rushing over him, around him, tingling deep inside. "Oh, God." He was so deep, so thick. And still moving, silently calling for more.

Another orgasm began before the first ended, and she was powerless to take a breath, for fear she might chase the feeling away. Her limbs tight and aching, she squeezed him with all her might, as he stroked her into the oblivion of pleasure, with it starting at her g-spot and shooting out from her core. Her nipples tingled, her fingertips numbed. The inner walls of her vagina quaked against the length of him, and a soft cry of satisfaction slipped through her lips.

"So passionate." He smoothed a curl at her temple, staring down at her.

She struggled to catch her breath. Tears curbed around her ears. "We can't keep doing this."

"I can't let you stop me." He cupped her body in his strong arms and pulled her onto his bare thighs. He removed her shirt and then his own.

The phone rang again, and she ignored it, their lovemaking continuing amid a tender embrace against the kitchen floor, Luke whispering into her ear. "This is it, what I've been waiting for my whole life."

* * *

"I have to go, Kimber," Luke said without looking at her. He pulled his snug T-shirt over his rippling stomach. "I want to peek in on my boy." His arms whisked into the denim outer shirt, which he didn't bother buttoning.

"Of course." Her brow furrowed as she dressed.

"Aw, don't do that, beautiful girl," he whispered, lightly brushing the crease at her forehead. "I can't stay. You know that."

"No, I know. I just thought you'd be...I don't know...happier about this."

"Happier? Believe me, I couldn't be any happier."

"You're...I don't know—"

"But this could be dangerous. For my kids, I mean."

"You don't think I stand to lose as much as you do? I have children, too, you know."

"Yeah, I know."

"Do me a favor. When you exercise your powers of persuasion, make damn sure you want to hit the target."

"What's that supposed to mean?" He pulled at a wrinkle in her shirt. "Here." He pressed her wedding ring into her hand.

"You have to be honest with me. If all you want is to fuck me—"

"You think that was fucking?" He reached for a shoe and shoved a foot into it. "Jesus, Mary, and Joseph."

"It wasn't fucking until you just treated it like fucking."

"I have to go. And you know I do."

"What do you want from me? Just sex?"

"It's never been about sex," he said, shrugging. "I mean, the sex is good, too. Incredible, but..." His gaze met hers, and he sighed.

"But what?"

"I have to go." He fingered a lock of her hair. "And you have to call your husband."

He kissed her softly on the mouth and disappeared out the door, leaving her feeling empty and easy.

And how insane had she been to do what she did with her husband on the line?

Had she turned off the phone?

Of course.

Had she?

Yes.

She looked again.

Yes. As a matter of fact, it had rung again, right? But what had her husband heard before she'd hung up?

She dialed Brennan's cell phone. "Hi."

"Are you all right?" Brennan asked.

"Yes."

"What happened, Kimmy?"

"Just a funny feeling inside."

"But you're all right?"

"Just pregnant. A little nauseous."

"Well, just a little longer, right? How long until the first trimester's over? And did you check the calendar for the fifteenth? Lauren and Rick are christening their home theater. Give my mother a call, see if she can take Allie, and maybe you can make that shrimp salad Lauren raved about a few weeks ago."

Tears filled her eyes. Back to reality. The magic of Luke Jackson faded like music on the wind.

* * *

Two days later, around six in the morning, she awakened with a terrific headache and a churning stomach. Good, a sign of pregnancy.

She forced herself out of bed, ready to vomit. Dizzy, she pinched her eyes closed and felt her way to the bathroom. When she felt the cool marble floor on the pads of her bare feet, she dropped to her knees and crawled. Finally, when she reached the closed door to the toilet room on the far side of the master bath, she reached up, turned the pewter door handle, and crept to the commode, the porcelain cooling her hot cheek.

The few contents of her stomach spewed into the toilet.

Ah. Pregnancy.

* * *

"But I can't find 'em, Mommy," Allison said from the breakfast room. "You have to look."

She peeled herself up from a snack bar stool and sauntered to her daughter's side. "What can't you find? Your bunny?"

"No. Pink is right here." Of course, sitting next to her ballet bag.

"What then, Allie?"

"Mommy, I told you. My noisy shoes that go shuffle, ball change."

"Your tap shoes?"

"Do tap shoes go shuffle, ball change?"

"Yes." *Okay. Where did you last see them?* Her hand fell to her abdomen for what seemed like the thousandth time that morning, her fingers dancing against it, a weak smile forming on her lips. She felt terrible. Terribly pregnant. If today weren't dress rehearsal for the recital, she would have spent the entire day in bed.

"Mommy? Are you sick?"

"I'm fine, Allie. And you know what? Your shoes are in my purse. Let's go."

* * *

"I wasn't going to say anything," Lauren said after half an hour of silence, "but, honey, you look terrible."

They sat side-by-side in the waiting room at the dance studio. Their daughters scampered off the maple floor, ready to switch from ballet shoes to taps, from one tutu to another.

"I'm not complaining today." Kimberley sighed and managed a smile. "I feel pregnant for the first time in weeks."

"Mommy." Allison shuffled toward her, taking care to tap her toes and heels against the floor with every step. Her hand outstretched, she offered up a gold object. "This was in my shoe."

Kimberley rose from her seat and took what she assumed to be part of a Happy Meal toy from her daughter's pudgy fingers. But when Allison pressed it into her hand, a bead of cold sweat formed on Kimberley's forehead.

Luke's wedding band.

Had Lauren seen it? Was there any excuse for having another man's wedding ring in her daughter's tap shoe?

Carefully, she tightened her hand around the ring. "Excuse me." She made her way to the restroom, locked the door behind her, and stared at her reflection in the mirror. An adulteress stared back at her.

The affair couldn't continue. It had to end.

She considered washing his cheap band of gold down the drain. He shouldn't have put it in her purse in the first place. She turned on the faucet, but before she allowed the ring to slip from her fingers, the picture on his dashboard entered her mind.

His ring, however inconvenient for her, was a symbol of the happiness portrayed in that photograph. Regardless of whether or not Luke deemed it necessary now, it had once meant a beginning without an end. She'd return it to him. In a public place, where nothing inappropriate could happen. At the gym maybe.

But there were no pockets in her sundress, and she'd neglected to bring her purse with her into the bathroom. Sandals wouldn't conceal it. Panic rose within her. What was she going to do with it?

She'd have to confess the lurid truth. She'd tell Lauren, and in turn, Brennan, that she had, safe in her keeping, a ring that not only belonged to another man, but a band of gold that had been inside her body, along with nine other digits and seven-and-five-eighths of pure man.

Her eyes darted around the bathroom. Could she wrap it in a square of toilet tissue? In a paper towel? And then what?

What was she going to do?

Out of the corner of her eye, she noticed her bra strap peeking out of her dress, and quickly, she shoved it back under. And suddenly, she knew what to do. She tucked Luke's ring between her full breasts and into the left cup of her bra. Its presence there, like its owner's, stimulated her and sent a vibration straight to her clit. Diane had married him, but his wedding ring pressed against Kimberley's breast, confined in her bra.

She splashed freezing water onto her face, feeling better. But deep down, she knew she had to end one of the two relationships in which she was involved.

"Why don't you go home?" Lauren said when Kimberley returned to her seat.

"I'm fine, Lauren."

"Are you?" She drummed her fingers against her Prada handbag, glancing at her, unable to hold the gaze. "Brennan called Monday night. It was pretty late. Around ten."

Kimberley's mouth dried instantly.

"He was worried about you, said you acted strangely on the phone."

Again, her courtroom experience leapt to her rescue. *Don't let her see your surprise. Act as if you're expecting every sentence she utters.* "Yeah. The morning sickness started again right around the time he called."

"Oh. Well, he asked me to check on you, so I called, but you didn't answer. And given the baby's heartbeat, I was worried. I sent Rick for a drive."

A long pause. "He didn't stop in."

"No, he said the house was dark, but nothing looked out of the ordinary. And the gateman said no one had come through, so he didn't want to alarm you or get you out of bed to answer the door."

Had Rick seen Luke's work truck parked on the road? Thank God Luke hadn't pulled into the drive that night. She'd have to tell him to leave his truck at Satchel Park next time.

Next time?

"So you were all right?" Lauren asked. "Just pregnant?"

There couldn't be a next time, no matter how amazing making love with him had been, no matter that she'd probably long for him every time she undressed. It was a dangerous game. And she couldn't play it.

She kept her poker face straight and dry. "Fine." Luke's wedding ring seemed to burn into her breast. "Just pregnant."

* * *

Rachael shyly took her pseudo-father's hand, and they filed out of the auditorium at Evanston High School.

"Did you like the show?" Luke asked.

She nodded silently.

About four feet to their right, Kimberley slowly made her way toward the door, her hand tucked in Brennan's arm. Her husband, a good-looking guy, kind of preppy, chatted with another couple.

"I wish Mommy were here."

Luke looked down into Rachael's wide, blue eyes, which were nothing like his. "Let's stop for some ice cream."

"Can we have ice cream at home?"

"Sure." One grueling step at a time. "Hey, we spend a lot of time together, right?"

"With Mommy."

"But we have more time together than most daddies and their girls, right?" He squeezed Rachael's hand and glanced at the Rodericks. Case in point.

"So, are you up for drinks after we get the girls?"

He overheard Brennan's suggestion, and his heart ached for Kimberley. His angel.

Her shoulders sagged, and she looked around the crowded hall, as if searching for someone to save her. She caught sight of Luke and snapped her eyes back for a second look, her initial look of pleasant surprise hardening immediately to something akin to nervous rage.

He'd invaded her world. Maybe he ought to have taken Diane's advice and stayed home, saved Rachael a hell of a lot of discomfort, and saved Kimberley the panic.

"Are you all right with that? I'll just have a couple. I'll be good." Brennan patted her delicate hand, the hand that had stroked Luke's balls.

Kimberley painted on a smile for her husband. "Fine. Allie's class will be in room one-seventeen. This way." She looked at Luke one last time before heading in a separate direction.

Luke turned his attention back to his daughter. "Would you like to take dance lessons someday?"

"Did Mommy take dance lessons when she was a little girl?"

"No, but doesn't it look like fun?"

"Yeah."

"Would you like to?"

"Do I have to, Daddy?"

He shook his head. "No."

* * *

"I'm making an appointment with the vet," Diane said the moment Luke walked in the bedroom door. "I'm putting him down."

"Rachael wants you to tuck her in," Luke said, pulling his shirt from his waistband.

"He pissed all over the carpeting in the family room."

"I'll clean it up." He fell onto the bed.

"What, do you think I haven't?"

"Our baby girl wants you."

"I mean it, Luke. He's gone. The moment you leave him in this house, in my care, he's out of his misery."

"Rachael wants you."

"Abysmal existence." Diane slammed her sock drawer and stood like a flamingo, pulling socks over her feet. "And by the way, your ring is nowhere in your office. Why don't you tell me the truth? Tell me you don't want to wear it anymore."

"Do I have reason not to wear it, Diane?"

"I'm putting that dog down. You'd best take him with you every time you leave, or he's history." She stormed out of the room.

Luke closed his eyes, picturing Kimberley Roderick in the long, black gown she'd worn to the evening's event. Elegant. Beautiful. Faking it for her husband, pretending to be the perfect wife, when less than a week ago, she'd creamed in his lap, kissed him as if tomorrow would never come.

If only he could have stopped time at that moment...

If he knew where it grew, he'd pick her a pocket full of clover, to keep her as lucky as she deserved to be. And with any luck at all, she'd share it with him. The way she'd shared it in her kitchen.

CHAPTER 13

On his way from a jobsite to the Cook County Counseling Center, Luke's cell phone rang for the eighteenth time in the past hour. What now? "Luke Jackson," he answered, certain his most unreasonable client had thought of another item for his punch list.

"Hi, Luke."

The sound of Kimberley's voice sparked him, convinced him momentarily to forget the hellish morning he'd endured. "Hi, beautiful girl."

"We need to talk. Can you meet me?"

He glanced at the clock. "With pleasure. I've got a meeting, but how about in a couple of hours?"

"I was hoping we could meet now. I'll be taking Allie to playgroup, and—"

"I'm on my way to the County Center. I have an appointment—"

"I won't take up much of your time."

"Take up as much as you wish. I don't want to hurry with you." How much time would cunnilingus take? Would she have time to return the favor?

"So is now good?"

"Yeah, if you can meet me outside the main building."

"I'll be there in ten minutes."

"Be careful. The roads are slick from the rain."

"It's raining?"

"Don't you ever look out the window?"

"Of course, but it's been a busy morning, and I've been... Never mind. I'll be there soon."

Eight minutes later, she pulled up beside his truck, and with as good as she looked, he had half a mind to take her up to Schaeffer's office and make love to her on the pipsqueak's coffee table.

"What were you doing there?" A tiny crease formed in her brow as she slammed the door of her SUV.

Her black, double-breasted raincoat cinched at her waist with a silver buckle, and her crimson red lips matched the fire in her eyes. High-heeled, open-toed sandals clapped against the wet pavement as she made her way to his truck.

"I took Rachael—"

"Aren't there other dance studios and other recitals?" She refused to take her eyes from his and yanked the door open. At last, she stopped moving when she realized Derby nearly filled the entire cabin. She smiled, and a giggle escaped her pretty mouth.

"Derby, you remember my angel," he said, gently shoving the dog's hind end off the seat. "Come on, boy, make some room."

Half the golden mass slid to the floor, but Derby's head remained planted on his master's lap.

Kimberley climbed in and patted the pup's head.

Would Derby recognize her scent? The Discovery Channel had recently run a report on dogs as eye- and nose-witnesses to crimes. Chances were the canine was more suspicious of the clues lingering in the threads of Luke's clothing than Diane.

"He's such a sweetie," Kimberley said. "He suits you."

"We suit each other." If her hand slipped from Derby's head, she'd rub something else. "I've had him since high school."

"Look," she said, her voice now softened, "you have to understand something. I've never been to your place. I don't know your home phone number. I've never seen your children, and there's a good reason for all of that."

"I understand."

"If we're caught, we're caught on my turf. And it's over for me. But you can carry on, your world undisturbed."

"If we're caught, I'm going down with you." He reached across Derby and held Kimberley's hand.

"So why were you there?" she asked softly, staring at their hands.

"I wanted to see Allie dance. I wanted Rachael to see a recital, and...I knew you'd be there, with your husband, and I wanted to see the two of you together."

"Why?"

"I want to know that you're all right. If I can't have you, beautiful girl, someone should be taking good care of you."

"Did you see the flask he was sipping on during the recital?"

He shook his head.

"Embarrassing."

"I'm sorry."

"I'm all right. I have to learn to live without you, but I'm all right."

He kissed her hand. "If I were your husband, I'd sip on nothing but you."

"I have to go."

"No, you don't."

"You have an appointment."

"I don't care about the appointment. I'm not going, and neither are you."

Her glance flitted from their hands to the scar at his eye, and back again. "Why do I feel this way when I'm with you?"

"And how is that?"

"This is wrong. Nothing about us is right, but the way I feel around you..."

With a finger on her chin, he drew her attention and planted a kiss on her lips.

"Is it because he doesn't make time for me? Is it because he can't keep a promise when it comes to over-indulging? Because he'd rather gamble away fun money than allow me to earn my own? Or is there something more here? Something more between us?"

"I'm sorry I brought Rachael to Allie's recital." He wove a hand into her curly hair. "I'm sorry I interrupted your night, and I'm sorry I tried to share something with my girl." He thought of the way Rachael had nervously shifted in her seat, like she had to go to the bathroom, but was afraid to tell him. "She likes to spend time with her mother, and Diane wants to be damn sure she doesn't trust me." His lips brushed against hers.

"She wouldn't do that, Luke. No mother in her right mind would."

"Diane's not necessarily in her right mind when it comes to me. Every day is a battle, and our children are the prize."

She closed her eyes and pressed her cheek to his hand. "You're a good father."

"You think I'm a good father."

"I know you are."

"Would you like to meet Caleb?"

Her lower lip fell a fraction of an inch, and she snapped her eyes open, shaking her head.

He cleared his throat. "Yeah, you're right. I guess it's not really—"

"If it's done in the right way, maybe."

He smiled. "Maybe." His hand slid to her stomach.

"Leave her."

Her abundantly clear request shocked him into silence for a few seconds.

"God, I can't believe I'm saying it, but—"

"You want me to leave her?"

"You should. You keep touching me."

"What if I promise not to anymore?"

"If you're not happy, you should leave her."

He rubbed his nose against her neck, inhaling her clean scent. "I don't know if I can do that."

"It's flattering to know that a woman so cold, so indifferent, so immune to your charm seems a more viable option than I do."

"As flattering as your choosing over me a gambling alcoholic who doesn't appreciate you."

"Noted."

He determinedly massaged over her pelvis. "Have you scheduled the ultrasound?"

"No."

"I'll go with you."

"I know, I just…" She pulled away. "I've been feeling pregnant again. That's a good sign."

"Yes, it is."

"You're missing your appointment," she whispered.

"I can still make it."

Kimberley looked down at Luke's companion. "What about Derby? Does he go with you?"

"I'll leave the truck running. He'll wait for me."

"Want me to take him? You can pick him up when you're done."

"That's all right."

"I don't mind."

"He's old and smelly. He'll dribble on your kitchen floor."

"Hey, you know what? Allie occasionally dribbles on the floor, and I've cleaned chunks of my husband's stomach out of the sink. I really don't mind."

* * *

"You're late," Schaeffer said, looking at Luke over the thin rims of his glasses. "I'd written you off again."

"Well, give me credit for this one." He dropped into the usual chair. "I'm here."

"Counseling is a commitment. If you can't commit to being here—"

"I'm here. I'm sorry I'm late."

"How are things going with the intimacy problem?"

"It isn't my problem. It's my wife's."

"It's your problem. Collectively."

"Look, I want it, I'm capable. She doesn't, and she's not. The only part that's my problem is that she's getting it somewhere."

Schaeffer snapped to attention, a look of surprise in his eyes. "Where do you get it, Mr. Jackson?"

"Don't worry about that. Worry about the positive pregnancy test I found in the trash. Worry about where Diane's getting it."

"You wanted to have an affair."

Luke nodded. Yes, and he'd chosen the right woman, who'd taken his dog, not only for the afternoon counseling session, but until he finished work for the day.

"You aren't wearing your wedding ring."

"If your wife were pregnant—again—with another man's child, would you be wearing yours?"

* * *

"I want to keep him," Allison said, lying across Derby's belly on the powder room floor.

"Allie, we can't. He belongs to another little boy and girl." As did Luke. Kimberley spun his wedding ring around her thumb. "Now, come on, brush your teeth. Time for bed."

"I don't like these pajammies."

"All right, let's change them."

"Really?" The little girl shot up, alert, relieving the dog of her weight.

"Mommy doesn't feel good enough to argue about it." The doorbell rang.

Allison looked toward the foyer. "Who's that?"

"Probably Derby's dad."

"When's my daddy coming?"

"Tomorrow." Kimberley walked into the foyer, her head aching. "After you go to sleep tonight, wake up tomorrow, and watch *Madeline*, Daddy will be home." Kimberley opened the door to a weary hunk of man. "Come on in."

"How did it go?" Luke asked amid a yawn, tapping a hand against his thigh. "Come here, boy."

"We're keeping him," Allison said, emerging from the powder room.

"Allie, say good night to Mr. Jackson and goodbye to Derby."

She crossed her arms and stuck out her lip. "I like him, and I want to keep him."

"Allie…" Kimberley sighed, rubbing her temples. "Luke, can you give me a few minutes? I'm just putting her to bed."

Luke crouched, and the dog wandered over to him. "What's that, Derby? You want Allie to kiss you goodnight?" He looked up. "What do you say, Allie?"

Her high ponytail bounced when she ran to embrace the dog. "Night-night, Derby."

"Maybe," Luke said, "if it's all right with your mommy, he can come play again someday."

"Really? Can he, Mommy?"

"I think that'd be all right. Now, come on upstairs to brush your teeth."

"And change pajammies?"

"And change pajamas. Come on." She spun the ring around her thumb.

A few minutes later, with Allison tucked into bed, Kimberley approached Luke. "Sorry about that."

"Hmmm." He smoothed a curl off her forehead. "She's such a pretty little girl." He nipped her lips. "With a sexy mama." His fingers caressed her hand, raking against his own wedding band, perched on her thumb.

"I didn't know I had it," she said. "I would've told you, but I just found it."

For a split second, his eyes fell on his ring, but he looked away without taking it back. He lowered her to the granite floor, cold on her back, and enveloped a breast beneath her T-shirt. A callus where his wedding ring used to be rubbed against her flesh, when he shoved the garment out of the way.

Derby turned his back and plopped onto the floor in front of the door.

"You weren't going to touch me," she said. "You promised."

"I lied." He lowered his mouth to her breast, his tongue encircling her nipple, his lips rolling seductively over her skin.

"I can't, Luke."

"Neither can I." He turned a cheek to her bosom, wiggling a hand into her pants.

The hard floor gnawed at her back, and his mouth landed on hers in a kiss in which his tongue softly caressed and relaxed hers, working her body with ten digits, his tongue, and her mind.

She clenched her fingers around his wedding ring.

"I don't have a choice," he whispered onto her lips. "I have to be inside you." His voice wavered, and his fingers slowly pressed into her vagina again.

"We can't—"

"What if I agreed to leave her?"

"You can't do that for me. I was wrong to ask."

He brought one hand to her cheek and continued to work her with the other. "She doesn't want me, beautiful girl. How can I live with a woman who doesn't want me?" His eyes pleaded, and he looked so young, so naïve, so in need of her, that she wanted nothing more than to please him. "Kimberley, please."

She dragged a finger along the fourth finger of his left hand. "I wish I'd met you before."

"You know me now."

She pulled his hand from her face and forced his wedding ring back onto his finger.

His little finger pressed into her one last time before he pulled his hand from her panties.

"Your children mean everything to you," she said. "Remember what's important."

"Someday, I'm going to explain all this to my boy, and he'll understand the way I feel about you."

"You don't know how you feel about me."

"Yeah, I do."

"No, you don't."

"I..." He clamped his mouth shut and looked away.

"You want to fuck me."

He yanked his ring off his finger. "This has never been about sex.

Well, maybe it was, but it isn't now."

"Then what's it about?"

"It's about us. About you and me. About the way I feel."

"You don't feel—"

"Don't tell me how I feel." He shoved his ring into his pocket. "I..."

"You...what?"

"I shouldn't say it."

"Don't worry about hurting me. Just say it. You want a no-strings-attached sex object."

"That's not what I want." He looked away. "And for the very last time, I don't think you're an object."

"What do you want then?"

"I don't know why I want what I want. Don't think for a minute that I haven't struggled with why I want it." His gaze shifted away, but quickly darted back.

"You see? You don't know."

"Maybe I just can't say it. Did you ever think of that?"

"Just say it. Tell me you need me for one thing, but you don't need me for—"

"I love you."

A smile crept onto her face. He was kidding, of course. "You do not."

Instantly, his cheeks flushed. "I should go." He backed away.

"What? Why? Luke, I'm sorry." She grasped his left hand. "I don't know what to say."

"I should go."

"I don't want you to go."

"Well, you don't want me to stay, and if this is what you want—this house, this man, this life—I don't want to tear your world apart."

"Luke, it never occurred to me that you might—"

"I don't expect anything from you. Just spend some time with me every once in a while, all right? Maybe lunch every now and again. So I don't forget how pretty you are."

From her position on the floor, she watched him walk away, longing for just one minute more with his arms around her.

With a hand pressed to her back—she felt a bruise coming on—she crept up the stairs, checked on her gorgeous, sleeping daughter, and fell into bed.

* * *

Luke sucked the fading taste of Kimberley from his fingers and entered his home. A packed duffel bag sat on the table, and his wife, sans wedding ring, read in her favorite recliner.

"I won't ask where you've been," she said, without taking her eyes from the pages, "if you turn right around and go back there."

He continued on to the family room and sat on the rug in front of her. "I'm not going anywhere."

"Who is she?" Diane set aside the book, glaring at him.

"What do you care, Diane?"

"Are you having an affair?"

"Is this what it's going to take to have it out?"

"Answer me."

He licked his lips and nodded. "Yes, I am."

"Then take your bag and go back to her." She reached for her book.

"I'm not going anywhere." He flung the paperback across the end table and stared hard into her eyes. "I'm done playing this game, Diane. You've been pushing me for years, and I'm done. But I'm not going anywhere."

"I can call the police and have you physically removed, if you'd like, but I'm giving you a chance to go."

"I'm not leaving my children."

"Don't you mean your *child*?"

"Rachael's mine, too, and it's your turn to go. Take your positive pregnancy test and go, but you're not taking my children."

"Do you think I'd leave them with you?"

"Do you think I'd let you out that door with them?"

"Your bag is packed, and in sixty seconds, if you aren't one foot out the door, I'm calling the police."

"Great. Tell them you're knocked up, tell them it isn't your husband's, tell them—"

"What's 'knocked up'?" Caleb's inquiry instantly silenced the room.

"Caleb, I—"

"Your dad and I are in the middle of something, Caleb. Go back to bed."

"Dad?" Caleb eyed the bag on the table. "Are you leaving us again?"

"I'm not going anywhere. I'll be up to tuck you in soon."

Caleb dawdled in the doorway. "Whose bag is that?"

"I'll be up in a minute. I promise."

The boy sighed heavily and finally turned back toward the stairs. When he was out of sight, Luke turned to his wife. "What do you think he heard?"

"The worst of it. Watch what you're saying."

"Ready to come clean with me?"

"There's nothing to say, Luke."

He pressed his lips together and nodded. "Okay. Give me a few days to get things ready at Julie's, and…" He shoved a hand through his hair. "Christ, let's be cooperative about this. Fifty-fifty, joint custody, all right? And I'll give you maintenance, if you want."

She shook her head. "I don't want to separate the children—"

"Neither do I."

"And since Paul's—"

"I don't want to hear about Paul Radcliffe. Where's he been the past five years? Was he there when I cut her umbilical cord? Was he there when she took her first step? When she said her first word? When she cried at the door on her first day of school? That gorgeous baby girl up there is mine. You aren't taking her."

"Damn it, she doesn't even like you, and you…you don't know the first thing about raising her."

"I know how to raise her just fine, and you know that. For once, Diane, think about our children." He stood, retrieved the book, and handed it back to her. "I'm going to say goodnight to Caleb."

CHAPTER 14

The sun had yet to rise when Kimberley sat up in bed, pressing her hands to her pounding forehead. "Ooh." One hand flew to her agitated abdomen. She swung her legs over the side of the bed and inched toward the bathroom.

Bile rose halfway up her throat and she barely made it to the commode. With her purging, she felt a dampness in her panties. What was that? Did she have to pee? Wasn't it a little early in pregnancy to lose urine?

With closed eyes, she yanked down her panties and sat. She felt a thick, mucus-like ooze gush out of her body and hit the water. She glanced into the bowl and saw only blood.

"Oh, God." Tears came instantly. She was miscarrying. "Okay, okay. It's okay."

She fashioned a pad out of toilet paper—*shouldn't use tampons*—and stuck it into her panties to absorb more of the blood. But her panties were already soaked with uterine lining.

Upon returning to bed, she found a dark red stain on the sheets, and looking down, she realized her nightgown, too, had been soiled.

She stripped the bed, slipped out of her nightgown, dressed in a bulky sweatshirt and underwear reserved for that time of the month, and headed to the laundry room, the bloody mess piled in her arms.

With a slow and disciplined gait, she thought of Luke's breathing with her at the doctor's office and exhaled her way through the pain. *Deep breath in, two, three, four, and out, two, three, four.*

At long last, she reached the upstairs laundry room and tossed the load in.

She pulled a pile of old towels—the ones she kept for the cleaning service—from a shelf in a custom linen cabinet, and after a long trek back to her bedroom, piled them atop her bed, fashioning a mattress guard she could lie down on.

She reached for the phone and dialed her doctor's office. "This is Kimberley Roderick. I'm thirteen-and-a-half weeks pregnant, and I'm having a miscarriage." The nurse on call relayed instructions.

Next, she called Lauren, who arrived within twenty minutes with Extra Strength Aspirin—Brennan had packed their home supply, for the likely event he'd have to nurse a hangover out of town—and a box of Super Maxis.

Kimberley swallowed three aspirin and pressed a pad into her panties. "Thanks, Lauren."

"Are you sure you won't let me drive you?"

"No, you have to get home to the kids before Rick leaves for work."

"He can take the morning off, Kimmy. You shouldn't drive yourself."

"This isn't your responsibility. If anyone should be missing work…" Kimberley stifled a sob. "You're doing more than enough."

*　　*　　*

A D&C was an unplanned abortion. She didn't want to admit it, but in listening to the nurse's explanation of what was about to occur within her body, Kimberley couldn't help drawing the parallel. This baby had already died, but through a medical procedure, its body would be removed much in the same way Jason's child had been, years ago.

"You won't be able to drive after," the nurse said. "We need to call someone to pick you up."

Kimberley rattled off Luke's cell phone number.

"And that's whose number?"

"A good friend. Luke Jackson."

"Just a few more questions, Mrs. Roderick."

"Questions about what? I've already told you everything I can think to tell you."

"Just routine, for clinical documentation."

"I don't want to talk about it. I just want it to be over."

"I understand, but your answers will help us give you the best possible care."

Kimberley nodded, wishing she had a hand to hold.

"Have you ever had a miscarriage before?"

"No."

"This is your second pregnancy?"

"Third."

"Any problems with the previous two?"

She looked away. "I ended the first. The second was fine."

"Have you been abused during this pregnancy? Emotionally, physically, sexually?"

She pressed her lips together. Had she been abused? By whose definition?

The nurse grasped her hand. "It's routine. What you say here stays here."

"I haven't been abused."

"You have several bruises on your legs, and one on your back."

No doubt, a product of sex against the kitchen island, foreplay in the foyer. "I bruise easily."

"For no reason?"

"I'm sure there's a reason. Maybe I bumped into a coffee table. I just don't remember."

"Are you anemic?"

"I don't know. I don't think so."

"How have you been eating?"

"Fine."

"Women who aren't normally anemic can become anemic if they fast, or if they don't follow a proper diet during pregnancy."

"I've been eating." But she'd missed many meals due to Brennan's sub-par Saturday morning conditions and secret meetings with Luke in the forest preserve.

"Have you been experiencing excessive fatigue?"

"I'm tired all the time. I'm always tired during the first trimester."

"We'll test your cell count. Fatigue is another symptom of anemia. When did you last have intercourse?"

She hesitated. Would Brennan ever see this record?

"Sometimes, Mrs. Roderick, intercourse stimulates uterine contractions. That's not likely the reason you lost this baby, but it might help explain why your body chose to expel it at this particular time."

"A few days ago."

"Any spotting afterward?"

"No."

*   *   *

Through sleep-filled eyes, Luke read six-o-eight on the clock. He rolled over, feeling for Diane, knowing she wouldn't be there. His wedding ring, however, perched on her pillow. He picked it up and spun it around the tip of his little finger.

What the hell was she trying to say? That she wanted him to wear it again? Just an ordinary morning, was that what he was supposed to think? Did she expect him to forget the evening of purgatory they'd shared? Never. He'd never forget the moment of clarity, when he'd realized his marriage was over.

The shrill of his cell phone jolted him from the ludicrous consideration. He swung his legs over the side of the bed and answered the phone. "Hello? Speaking." He tossed his ring onto the bedside table and hung his head while Evanston Northwest Hospital personnel confirmed his worst fears regarding his beautiful girl's pregnancy. "I'll be there as soon as I can."

After an abbreviated morning routine, he hurried to the kitchen for a quick cup of caffeine. But Diane hadn't brewed the coffee yet. He opened the pantry and located a filter and the coffee canister. Now he was about to be single again, he should probably get used to doing things on his own anyway. Folding his laundry, sweeping his own dirt out the door, clearing the table.

He looked up. Diane had always taken care of those things. Six-thirty in the morning, and the kitchen was spotless. And the duffel bag was gone. And so was she. "Hell."

He threw together some lunch items and rushed up to his son's room. "Caleb."

His son's eyes opened. "Hi, Dad."

"Come on, buddy. Aunt Julie's going to get you off to school this morning."

"Why?" Caleb yawned.

"I have an emergency."

"Is Rachael coming?"

Panic. Had Diane taken his little girl? He hadn't yet checked her room. He cleared his throat. "Yes. Come on, grab your things."

"Why can't Mom take me to the bus?"

"Mom had a rough night and she needs some time."

"Because you were fighting again?"

"Get dressed and brush your teeth."

Caleb groaned and rolled out of bed.

Luke swept into the next room, relief washing through him while he ran a hand over his daughter's flannel-clad back. "Rachael."

"Hmmm." The little girl's sigh sent satisfied tingles up and down his arms.

"Wake up, Rae-rae."

Slowly, her eyes peeled open. "Hi, Daddy."

* * *

In a pale yellow room, Kimberley awakened to see Luke sitting with his head in his hands in a chair opposite her recovery bed, a T-shirt—torn at the collar—clinging to his body. "Thanks for coming." Her words escaped her much more quietly than she'd expected, but Luke snapped to attention.

He half-smiled. "Hey, beautiful girl."

She ran a hand through the mop of frizz atop her head. "Don't look at me."

"You're beautiful."

"You're too kind."

"Kimber"—he rubbed a callus on his thumb—"I can't pretend to understand what you're going through, but if it helps you, I feel like it's my loss, too." He looked away, sighing. "I'm sorry."

Tears welled in her eyes and she blinked them away. "I guess I got what I deserved, didn't I?"

"You know this isn't your fault. It's God's way of weeding out babies who can't make it." His eyes settled on her, and she softened under his scrutiny. "I wish I'd been there. To help you."

She shook her head, imagining the mess his being there would've caused. She would have bled all over him, Lauren would have arrived, finding him there…

"You're right, Kimber. I didn't have to be there, but that son-of-a-bitch you married should've been."

"He's traveling."

"Yeah, I know." Luke rose from his seat and paced about the room. "And if he happened to be home, he'd be preoccupied with who's leading in the seventh inning, the money he has riding on it, and the bottle of whiskey getting him through it all."

"I've learned to handle things like this on my own."

"And that makes it okay?" He frowned. "You can't be fulfilled, living like this. I mean…" He stopped at the foot of her bed and stared at her. "Are you?"

"Fulfilled? There's plenty wrong with my marriage, Luke, but I have to try."

"You ever going to be tired of trying?"

"I don't know. Are you?"

He rubbed his eyes with the thumb and forefinger on his left hand. Still no wedding ring. "She left. When I woke up this morning, she was gone."

"Oh, my God," she said softly, "how are you holding up?"

He sat on the edge of her bed. "I'm all right. She left the children, so—"

"Come here."

He leaned to her, pressing a hand to her stomach. "Don't worry about me. Concentrate on getting better."

"About last night." She squeezed his hand. "About what you said."

"You shouldn't be thinking about that right now."

"It means a lot to me. But it hit me out of the blue, and I suppose I reacted poorly."

"Don't worry about it."

"And about this." She tickled his bare ring finger. "You would've taken it off sooner or later, whether or not you ever met me."

"Maybe." His brow furrowed. "But as things turned out, I took it off because I met you."

"Why do you think you love me?"

"I don't think it, I know it."

"But doing this is too hard. We can't—"

"You're upset. But don't worry, beautiful girl. You'll be pregnant again in no time. With my baby, and my babies hold on."

"I can't—"

"It doesn't have to be this crazy. It can be as simple as two people giving each other what they need. No one expects you to stay with him, if you aren't happy." He brushed his thumb over her fingers. "And I don't expect you to do anything right now but heal."

"Do you really think you might love me?"

His smile illuminated the room. "I know I do."

*   *   *

Lauren held her hand as Kimberley spoke into the phone. "Brennan, how was your flight?"

"Flight was fine. Week was a little hellish. I stopped off for a round with the Oakbrook team. I'll be home after the game. Looking good for me, Kimmy. Seventy-five if Garciaparra gets on base again, one way or another."

"You have to come home."

"I said I'd be home soon."

"Now." Although she tried desperately to contain it, a sob escaped her.

"What's wrong?"

"I… Bren, I lost the baby."

"How? How did this happen?"

"Brennan, I don't know."

"What happened? Was it the exercise? The eating? Or was it something to do with…what happened before we met?"

"Just come home, okay?"

"I'll be on my way soon."

"I'm sorry, Bren."

"So am I."

* * *

"Where are my babies?" Luke patted Derby on the head and made his way into his sister's kitchen.

Julie rubbed her pregnant belly. "With Bobby in the back yard. Are you hungry?"

"No, but I'll eat." He pecked his sister on the cheek.

"It's nothing fancy. Tuna noodle casserole."

Derby followed him to the table, where Luke sat, yawning. "Thanks for filling in at the last minute."

"I don't know how Diane does it. They're a lot of work. And…Luke, Derby's not looking so good."

"He's hanging in there."

"And you?"

"Me, too."

"Why haven't you been wearing your wedding ring?"

"We had it out last night. There's not much left of us." He looked up at his sister, rubbing a thumb over an eye, smiling. "You sure make me look like a failure, you know that? You've got it all together here."

"We have problems, just like anyone." She turned back toward the kitchen. "You try, you work on it. You forgive."

"I've forgiven all I can." Derby collapsed on Luke's feet beneath the table, settling in for an evening nap. "I wonder if this is how Dad felt."

"Don't even start, Luke."

"No, really. Maybe he gave up, just like I did."

* * *

Kimberley glanced at the clock—after ten o'clock and still no word from her husband. She opened her wedding album, lamenting what she and Brennan could have been. Not that she blamed the disintegration of their marriage solely on him. She'd done plenty to help its erosion. All the looking away, all the enabling...Luke.

The phone rang. She answered before checking the Caller ID, prepared to hear Brennan's slurring voice on the line, asking if she minded him having another drink before he headed home.

"Kimberley Roderick?"

"Yes."

"This is Officer Teague with the Cook County Police Department."

She slumped into the sofa, gripping the photo album for support. "Yes?"

"Are you Brennan Roderick's lawyer?"

"I guess so. Also his wife."

She listened to the officer's commentary and thanked him when he had no further information. She hung up the phone and dropped her head into her hands. For three minutes, she whimpered, not knowing what else to do, but when she peeled her hands from her face, the first thing she saw was Brennan's drunken, smiling face staring up at her from the pages of her wedding album.

Family-shmamily. And he'd asked the officer to call his lawyer. Not his *wife*, but his *lawyer*.

Consumed by anger, she ripped expensive photographs from the leather-bound book and shoved them, bent and crinkled, into the fireplace. The next item tossed in to burn was a case of monogrammed poker chips. She opened drawers, found decks of cards and betting slips from Arlington Race Track. She stuffed it all into the box.

She charged to the corner of the room, cracked open the doors of the walk-up bar, and pulled out a bottle of whiskey. Through her tears, she spied a second bottle behind the first, and then a third.

She hurled the bottles into the fireplace—crash, crash, crash!—and watched the liquid soak through the mementos of her wedding day, and through the reminders if her husband's addictions. Shoulders shaking, her breath caught in her throat. She slid a long, blue-tipped match from the weathered tin on the limestone hearth, flared the match, and watched the fire fill the box instantly, catching on the whiskey-doused photographs.

CHAPTER 15

Her knuckles whitened with her tight grip on her cell phone, her heart racing. Officially, she'd gone out of her mind. But who better to confirm her insanity than—

"Jason?"

"Yes."

The delightful squeals of happy children sounded in the background. She smiled, despite the churn of jealousy in her stomach. "Hi, it's me. Kimberley."

Only dead air and static answered her. Just when she expected to hear the click of a terminated phone call, he said, "Kimberley Quinn Callahan?"

"Yeah, remember me?"

"I think so. Hi."

"Is this a good time?"

"After all these years, I'd say it's about time. How are you?"

"All right. And you?"

"You're a hard person to find, you know. You aren't listed anywhere, even under your new name."

He'd tried to find her? Whoa.

"It's good to hear from you," he said.

"I know this is short notice." She opened *The Fabulous Gourmet* and fingered the worn letter tucked into the hollandaise page. "Can you meet me for lunch?"

"Today?"

"I know it's short notice, but I'd really like—"
"Absolutely. Let me check with my wife, but—"
"—to talk to you."
"When and where?"
She smiled. "I'll make it very convenient for you."

* * *

A few minutes before noon, Kimberley approached Dot's Diner with hesitation, but she quickened her steps when she saw Jason refusing the Fish Bowl, an infant carrier swinging in a strong hand.

The years had certainly been kind. His eyes—deep forest green—had mellowed with age, tiny fine lines at the corners. A silvery gray dusted his blonde hair at his temples. But his hard body advertised Friday night softball games, mornings at the gym…and, more than likely, frisky evenings in bed.

"Hey, Kim." He embraced her with one arm. An awkward semi-hug.

"Thanks for meeting me," she whispered.

"Good to see you."

"You look great." She slid into the booth, nodding toward the infant carrier he'd placed on the opposite bench. "So who's your friend there?"

"This is my youngest, Clara."

She peered at the tiny, sleeping baby. "She's precious. How old is she?"

"Six weeks yesterday."

"Congratulations."

"Thanks."

A waitress dropped a couple of menus on the table.

"What do you think?" Jason glanced at her over his menu. "No, let me guess. Some sort of calorie-saving salad with a chocolate malt on the side."

"I'm still predictable after all these years."

"Not predictable. You're still you, and I'm glad to see that marriage hasn't changed you."

"I'll take that as a compliment."

"How's Brennan?"

"I'm surprised you remembered his name."

"Hard to forget that one."

"How's Linda?"

"Good. Thanks for asking." During a lull in the conversation, he fiddled with his baby's hat, finally removing it from her beautiful, round head.

"So how many children do you have? I heard them on the phone." His eyes sparkled, and he reached for his wallet. "Three. You?"

"Just one. A girl."

He deposited pictures of two small girls before her. "Christina just turned four, and Caitlyn's two."

"They're beautiful. You've been busy."

"And they'll keep me busy for a long time coming. Do you have pictures?"

"Yeah." She reached into her purse, set Allison's tap shoes on the table with a *clink, clink,* and produced a billfold of pictures. "I have her photographed at least once a month."

"How do you make time for that, what with your career and all?"

"I'm...I'm retired, Jason. I have been since I had her."

"Oh." After a moment, the disappointment in his eyes waned. "Good for you."

"She's worth it."

"She's a pretty little girl." He flipped through the pictures. "What's her name?"

"Allison Colleen."

He pointed to the tap shoes. "A River-dancer."

"Yes," she said with a chuckle. "She dances."

"So does Chrissy."

"Maybe we can get the girls together. Do this again some time."

"I'll run it by Linda, but why not?" He shrugged. "It was never my idea to quit you cold turkey."

Whoa, again. She traced the rim of her water glass. "Look, I know you're being polite, but let's call the balk, all right? You left me."

"Yeah." He looked away. "But we left each other all the time."

"Well the last exit was yours, through and through."

"You know why."

"Actually, I don't. I thought I knew, but then, the letter arrived. On the night before my wedding."

"I'm sorry about that. I shouldn't have—"

"No, it's fine. But you asked me to wait. Why, when you're the one who walked away?"

"I was angry, Kim, but that didn't mean I wanted you to marry someone else."

Her mouth fell open.

"A few months couldn't erase all those years. I guess I always assumed we'd...you know, get over it, and get back on track. Naïve, I know, but—"

"Jason, I'm sorry for what I did. And I know it would've meant much more had I said it a decade ago, but—"

"You had every right to do what you did."

"I know things happened quickly between Brennan and me, but believe me, Jason, I think about you—I think about us—all the time. About that crazy decision."

He shifted in his seat, his fingers fumbling with the canopy on the infant seat. "You shouldn't."

"Don't you wonder *What if?*"

"What is it," he asked with a smile, "with women and *What if?* The most strong-willed women in the world"—he pointed across the table—"Case in point...question their decisions."

"It was a hard decision to make."

"You made it look easy."

"I'm sorry you feel that way, but it was the most difficult decision I'd ever made."

He cleared his throat. "In this game of *What if*, do you ever wish you'd decided differently? Do you ever wish we'd had the baby?"

"That all depends on what might've happened later. Children need two parents."

"Didn't I tell you we'd work it out?"

"Well, yes, but—"

"We would've worked it out."

"In that case, do you ever wish you'd told me how you felt about it?"

"Yeah, I do. I look at her"—he nodded toward Clara—"and I think number four. Regardless of whether you wanted me, I wanted you to want that baby."

They stared soberly across the table at one another, while the waitress delivered their soup. Once alone again, Kimberley cleared her throat. "I wish I hadn't been so selfish, but I was young, so clueless. I didn't know what I had, how lucky I was to have it, but I know now."

"Don't we all?"

She blinked away the tears creeping into her eyes. "I just had a miscarriage."

"Kim, I'm sorry."

"I'm all right." She reached for a package of soda crackers. "Brennan and I have a lot to work through. Maybe it was just the wrong time."

"Does he know we're having lunch?"

"I'm going to tell him, but I haven't talked to him since yesterday. We're kind of...well...separated at the moment."

"Separated? What happened?"

And then she told him everything. About the money, the gambling. About Brennan's drinking and his most recent tirade behind the wheel of a car. About envying Lauren. About Allison's wardrobe rampages and the challenges of raising a child on her own. About the baby she lost. And she told him about...

"Luke." He repeated the name, as if committing it to memory.

"I don't know how it happened."

Jason directed his full attention to the navy bean soup before him.

"I know I can't live like this. I know something has to change."

He nodded but remained silent.

"Jason, say something."

"What do you want me to say?"

"Tell me you're disappointed, tell me you dodged a lethal bullet, tell me you're ashamed of me."

"I'm not, I didn't, and I never could be. You did what you had to do. In that clinic years ago, and now, with this other guy."

"You don't condone what I did. Don't pretend to."

He reached across the table and gave her hand a brief squeeze. "You'll work it out. One way or another."

* * *

"Did you call my lawyer?"

There's that word again. Lawyer.

Brennan's dirty hands hung out between the bars of the holding cell, his left hand twitching with the shakes. His wedding ring reflected the fluorescent light above him. "Well, if you called her, why isn't she here? This is ridiculous. I donated five times my bail to this organization last fall."

"I'm here," Kimberley said, quickening her pace toward the cell.

"You took your own, sweet time calling her, didn't you, Officer?"

"No." She approached the cage, which reeked of stale alcohol, and stopped just out of Brennan's reach. "They called last night."

"Coco Bop." He softened. "Kimmy, I'm sorry I didn't—"

"Shut up, Brennan."

He clamped his mouth shut and raked his crystal blue gaze over her.

"I needed you. While I was busy cleaning a dead fetus from my womb, you were at a bar, waiting for Garciaparra's next at-bat and your seventy-five dollars."

He grinned. "I got it, didn't I?"

"Let's get through the business part of this first, shall we?"

"Get me out of here, and we'll talk about it."

"One thing at a time." She turned to the officer on deck. "My client and I need to confer. Can we have a private room?"

The officer approached the cell, keyed in a pass code, and opened the door. "Right this way."

They followed him to a tiny concrete cell, and once alone, Brennan cleared his throat. "What do we have to discuss here that we can't talk about at home?"

She pursed her lips and raised her brows, reading him like a witness. If she neglected to speak, he would fill the silence.

"Jesus, what's wrong with me?" He pulled out a rusty folding chair. "How are you?"

She sat and opened her leather portfolio. "How am I indeed?"

"Did the doctor say when we could try again?"

"Why would you ask? It's not the right time, remember? Anyway, I have some thinking to do. I've just come from lunch with Jason—"

"Jason? Jason Devon?"

"He's doing well, said to say hello."

Brennan shook his head. "Have you heard? How's the guy who hit me? They won't tell me."

"First of all, it wasn't a guy. Secondly, are you sure she hit you?"

"That's the way I remember it."

"Are you sure?"

"I was fine to drive, Kimmy."

"They've got a point-one-six that says otherwise."

"Is she"—Brennan rubbed his hands together—"you know, all right?"

"And what would you feel if she weren't?"

"Kimmy?" At long last, he took the seat opposite her. "She's all right, isn't she?"

"Well, that's subjective. She's in the hospital, but she woke up last night, with no recollection of leaving the party she'd attended. She's eighteen, with a previous alcohol charge, and she blew a point-one-nine. The judge probably won't bat an eyelash at your B.A.C., seeing as this is your first offense."

"Second."

Her gaze met his. "Second?"

"It's off my record, I think. It was before I met you, in college. Ask Lauren. She'll know when."

More secrets, more connections between Lauren and her husband. "I'll look into it, but the fact of the matter is a point-one-six is still an inarguable D.U.I., Bren. Double the legal limit. You'll have to go to classes, and you'll have at least a hundred hours of community service. And if your first offense is public record, you could do jail time, considering Ms. Herman's condition."

"That's ridiculous." He beat his fist into his palm. "She hit me. I'd have been home, taking care of you last night, if only she'd handled her liquor."

"Brennan, if you'd come straight home from O'Hare, you'd have been home before the D and C was complete. At the very least, you should have left the moment I told you about the miscarriage. Don't blame your misfortune on the drinking of an eighteen-year-old kid."

"You have to bargain me down to a hefty fine. I don't have time for community service, and as far as serving time—"

"I can't bargain anything for you. These laws became pretty cut and dry the second you agreed to blow, and it's high time you learned you can't buy your way out of mistakes like this. Be thankful I don't suggest Gambler's Anonymous on top of it all."

"Whose side are you on?"

"Yours."

"Are you sure about that?"

"Would you like to call someone else?" She began to pack her papers into the portfolio. "The attorney-client relationship should be based on trust, and if you don't think I can do the job—"

"Of course I think you can do the job." He rose from the chair. "You'll get me time served. I'll have classes and community service."

"And you'll lose your license for a while."

"How long?"

"That's up to the judge, but six months is standard in this state."

"Six months? I think I'd rather do time."

"Compared to other states, that's a cake walk. A freebie. Across the state line you'd lose your privilege to drive permanently."

The echo of the old building's plumbing reverberated in the

concrete walls amid his silence.

"Do you have anything else to say?" she asked.

"Of course I do."

"Now's the time."

"I'm sorry, Coco Bop."

"I hate that nickname."

He sank back onto the rusting chair. "I know I made a mistake, with Garciaparra, with driving, but you have to believe me. I didn't think I was drunk. I only had a few."

"You had more than a few. You always do. But why, knowing that I needed you, did you take even one more sip? I should be able to rely on you, but how can I count on a man who loves gambling—and everything it leads to—more than he loves his wife?"

"I love you, Kimmy. I wish—"

"I'm not finished." She glared at him.

He clamped his mouth shut.

"I'm leaving you."

"I'll get help. You just said yourself that this time, I don't have a choice, so I'm getting help. Kimmy, think of Allie. And if the games and bets bother you to the point of your leaving, it's no question of what's more important to me. I'd never gamble away our marriage."

"You already have, and so have I."

"You're not leaving me. And that's that. We married for better, for worse, and—"

"Brennan, listen. This time, it isn't about you. It's about me."

"What about you? About the baby, you mean? The miscarriage?"

"Well, yes, that's part of it, but, Brennan—"

"We'll get through it," he said, pressing the heels of his hands to his eyes. "I've got some vacation time saved, and I'll take a leave of absence, maybe, while my license is suspended. We'll try again for another baby as soon as we can, get back on the horse and back on the track for the life we set for ourselves, for our family."

"Brennan, I'm having an affair."

He looked up, directly into her eyes. "You're lying."

"It started harmlessly enough. He was just someone who bent an ear, someone who—"

"Why are you saying this? It isn't true...it can't be."

"It's true."

"It's true?"

"Yes."

"You're fucking another man, and I'm put through the wringer for wagering a measly seventy-five bucks and having a few drinks last night?"

"I'm not fucking him." She watched him pace the cell. "It's worse than that."

"Worse? What could be worse that fucking your ex-boyfriend?"

"It isn't Jason."

"Who is it?"

"And I'm not fucking him, I'm...I'm holding his hand, and he's listening to me, and we—"

Brennan's fist met the cinder block wall at the back of the cell. "Who is he?"

"I never meant for it to happen, but—"

"Who is he?" He cradled his swelling hand and approached her.

She straightened, staring up at him with confidence, certain she was doing the right thing. "It doesn't matter."

"Yes, it does. Who is he?"

"He's a gentleman—"

"All evidence to the contrary."

"—by the name of Jack Daniels."

He squinted at her.

"Or Jack Binion," she continued. "Lauren and Rick, for that matter. Your job. I'm never first on your list, and neither is your daughter."

"Do you honestly mean to imply that I've driven you to this?"

She raised her eyebrows but said nothing.

"Give me a break."

"You can have the house," she said, "and everything in it. All I want is Allie and my mother's settee."

"You're not leaving me. We're in this together."

"But I'm the only one working on it, and I'm done."

"Are you done with him, too?"

"He's been there for me, he's helped—"

"But if you love me, and if you honestly never did anything, anything sexual—"

"I said I wasn't fucking him, but I'm not going to lie to you, Brennan. A lot happened."

"Was that baby even mine?"

"You know the answer to that question."

"But you had sex with this guy."

"I was pregnant when I met him."

"So you've stopped believing in us," he whispered. "That's why you did it. You don't believe in us anymore."

"Do you believe in us, Bren?"

"I believed in everything about us. I believed in you. I believed in our family. I loved you, but you ruined it, with this guy, this—"

"I beg your pardon? *I've* ruined it?"

"How can I forgive this? And you're so far gone, sleeping with other men, how could you want me to?"

"I don't expect or want your forgiveness. How do you think I got to this place? I didn't wake up one day and decide to hurt you, Brennan. We've been eroding for years and years. Do you ever think about whether you really *love* me, Brennan? Maybe you're just used to saying it."

He raised a hand to her cheek. "If I didn't believe in us, don't you think I'd take this ticket out of here? You gave me an excuse to leave, but—"

"You don't have to leave me. I'm going."

"—but I love you. You can't leave me for him."

"I'm not. I'm leaving you for me."

CHAPTER 16

Six months later

"So what kind of guy is Paul?" Luke asked as he drove down a snow-covered street. Derby's golden mass spilled over both his and Caleb's laps.

His son shrugged, staring out the window. "Can't play ball worth squat."

"But he's nice to you?"

"He's all right."

Luke dropped the plow and turned into a driveway alongside a two-story saltbox colonial, white, with black shutters. Kimberley's new place, less than half the size of the castle on Hidden Creek Lane, was still bigger than the home in which he and Diane had planned to retire. "Does Rachael like him?"

Again, Caleb shrugged. "Why are we doing this house?"

"Favor for a friend." Luke searched the windows of the large dwelling for his beautiful girl; he didn't see her. In fact, although they'd spoken a few times a week, he hadn't seen her since the day she'd miscarried. Her idea. Space. Time to think and do the right thing.

Well, he'd had enough of both.

"Dad?"

"Yeah, Buddy."

"Do you think Mom's going to marry Paul?"

"Yeah. She's having a baby. That usually means people love each other." He glanced at his son, who frowned and stared out the window. "Is that okay with you?"

"But you always come back."

His stomach flip-flopped. "Not this time."

"Is Mom right? Are you like your dad?"

"Caleb."

"Because Mom says that your dad—"

"If I were like my dad, I wouldn't pick you up from school or take you plowing. We wouldn't see each other the way we do. My dad left when I was five years old, and I didn't see him until I was grown up." At the top of the driveway, he shifted the car into park and looked his boy squarely in the eyes. "Your mom and I can't make it work, but that doesn't change you and me."

He heard a knock on his window and turned to see Kimberley, layered in a fluffy white turtleneck sweater and a beige jacket, with a steaming mug in her left hand. No mittens, no wedding band. A hint of a smile touched her lips. God, he'd thought she was beautiful last spring, but now...

Her hair, secured in a clip at the nape of her neck, cascaded down her back, her curls more relaxed than he remembered. The winter wind bit at her pink cheeks, and the tawny glaze on her lips tempted him beyond reason.

"Who is that?" Caleb asked. "Do you know her?"

"Used to." He zipped down the window. "Hi."

"I thought it might be you," she said, her smile brightening. "You're in and out before I go to work."

"I aim to please." On Tuesdays and Thursdays, the days she taught at UIC, he awakened before first light to clear her drive. "I'll be out of your way in about two minutes."

"What's this?" She smiled and gave him a playful tap at the crown of his head.

"This?" He pulled the fraying hood of his thick sweatshirt over his brow, revealing the frowning face Caleb had drawn in red marker on the top of his hood. "We get cranky when it's real cold."

"Aren't you cute?" Her nose wrinkled when she smiled. "I've been meaning to call. To thank you."

"Not necessary."

"Why don't you come in for a few minutes and warm up? Coffee? Hot cocoa?"

He'd love to warm up with her, that's for sure. He glanced at Caleb, who stared him down, as if he'd known his father's history with this woman. "Maybe some other time, Kimber. But thanks."

With a fading smile, she nodded. "All right. Here, take mine."

He accepted the mug, stained with fawn-colored lipstick, where she'd sipped it once or twice. He placed his lips upon the remnants of hers and drank. Just the way he liked his coffee—with sugar, and a drop of cream. Kind of like her kisses.

"Anything for Caleb?" she asked.

He turned to his boy, who shook his head. "No thanks."

"I'd like to pay you for your time," she said.

Of course she would. "Not necessary."

"No, really. You have no idea how much it helps. I'd have to leave Allie in bed, and—"

"You weren't made for shoveling."

"I'm capable, and your time is worth—"

"How about another cup of coffee sometime?" He remembered the first time he'd asked for a morning cup of joe—and the jolt he'd received that day had had nothing to do with caffeinated beverages.

She blushed—apparently, she remembered, too—and pulled the sleeves of her coat over her hands. "Anytime."

"You sure about that?"

After a hesitant nod, she hitched her chin up, bouncing a curl out of her eyes. "I think so." She smiled at Caleb before turning away, leaving the scent of her hair behind.

"How did she know my name?" Caleb asked.

"What?" Luke looked away from the snow angel who had long ago captured his heart.

"She knew my name."

"She knows all about you. Grab the shovel and get her sidewalk, will you?"

Caleb yanked his hood up, exposing the matching, frowning face on his sweatshirt, and wiggled out from beneath Derby's weight. By the time the boy was finished, Luke had cleared the driveway, and they headed back toward a tiny apartment on the edge of Des Plaines.

"Do you think that lady's pretty?"

Luke curbed an enthusiastic affirmation and settled for a "Yeah."

Caleb, silent, stared out the window at cars whizzing past in colorful blurs amid the snow.

"Why?"

The boy's shoulders jabbed upward. "I don't know. She seemed sad."

"She did?"

"Yeah."

Well, maybe he'd have to do something about that.

"Is she your girlfriend?"

"No."

"Mom says you have a girlfriend."

"Mom's wrong."

* * *

"Oh, hello, 8-8-2-3."

Kimberley smiled at the drycleaner and grasped Allison's hand. "How are you today?"

"Cold out, no?"

"Quite."

"Cold air put rosy glow on pretty face."

"Thank you."

"Oh, you beautiful, and have beautiful girl, too."

Allison hid behind one of Kimberley's legs.

"You hang tough, 8-8-2-3." She turned to Mr. Drycleaner, barked out several choppy syllables in Korean, and turned back to Kimberley. "Boys. They not know a good thing if it make them sneeze, no?"

Kimberley took the bagged suits—remnants from her single year of litigation, good enough for the classroom—and waved goodbye. "Come on, Allie. Let's get you to ballet class."

"Will Auntie Lauren be there?"

Kimberley's heart ached. She missed her friend, who had promised they'd keep in touch, but never returned her calls. Perhaps she should have moved further north, put more of a buffer between them. "Maybe."

"Can we have play group with Deacon and the girls?"

"How about with Chrissy, Caity, and Clara?"

"Maybe Daddy can take me to Auntie Lauren's. Do I go see Daddy soon?"

The wind whipped through Kimberley's hair and chilled her straight through her woolen coat. She tightened her grip on Allison's hand. "In a few days."

"When?"

"You have to go to sleep at night twice more, then Daddy will come get you."

"I miss Daddy."

"I'm sure Daddy misses you, too."

"Does Daddy miss you?"

If he did, he'd never told her so. Always civil, always sober when he arrived to retrieve his daughter for their every-other-weekend visits, he'd regarded Kimberley with indifference. Like she was just someone he used to fuck twice a week. Like she was a baby vehicle he was still paying for with state-garnished wages, although he probably figured he'd traded up with his new, brainless girlfriend.

The frigid air stung her cheeks, and she fought the impulse to break down. *Stay strong. For Allison.*

"Mommy?"

She opened the car door and stowed the drycleaning in the rear of her SUV. "Yes, baby?"

"I love you."

"I love you, too." She grabbed Allison's ballet bag from the backseat and led her daughter down the sidewalk to the Sugar Plum Studio, where she wrote a check for—ouch—two hundred dollars. Costume deposit for the spring recital.

* * *

"I saw that you called earlier." Luke held the phone tight to his ear, driving toward the County Counseling Center. "I'm sorry I missed you. Did you need something? Anything?"

"It was nothing important. I...I feel silly even saying this, but I bought you a few T-shirts. And flannels."

He'd bought something for her, too—a golden bracelet with a four-leaf-clover charm. It seemed silly now, and she was probably used to jewelry boasting precious stones, but maybe she'd like it, if he could gather the nerve to give it to her. "You didn't have to do that."

"You don't have to plow my driveway either, and if you'll forgive my saying so, you need new shirts. Everything you own is torn. At least it used to be."

"Occupational hazard."

"How's business?"

"Mad dash last month to finish everything before Thanksgiving, but now, slow."

"I'm sorry."

"It'll pick up in the spring."

"It was good to see you the other day."

"Hey." He drummed his fingers against the steering wheel. "Is Allison home?"

"No, it's Brennan's weekend."

"How about that? Our kids are on the same schedule. Could you use some company?"

"Do you think that's a good idea?"

"I think it's the best idea I've had in a long time." He pulled over to the side of the road, allowed the cars behind him to pass, and u-turned illegally. Derby groaned in his sleep next to him.

"I'm going to be candid with you, Luke."

"All right."

"It was good to see you."

"It was good to see you, too."

"And you look great. Life is obviously agreeing with you."

"You, too."

"I keep thinking about what you said to me that one day. You know, when you told me—"

"When I told you I loved you, yeah."

"I don't know if you meant it or not, but I think about it."

"I think about it, too."

"You always used to touch me. And not in the way that men touch women in the general sense, but you know…you used to really…touch me."

"Can I…can I come see you?"

"Don't go out of your way."

"I'm close."

"I think it might be too soon. I'm still pretty raw."

"How 'raw' can you be? You made the move."

"That doesn't make it easy. You should know that."

"Lonely, I'll buy. But raw? You'd been—"

"He's getting married next May. I'd say raw just about covers it."

"Oh, wow. I can understand that. Diane's due after the first of the year."

"Guess I was pretty easy to forget, huh?"

"No." He pulled into her driveway and retrieved a black velvet bracelet box from the glove compartment. He slipped the gift into the pocket of his insulated flannel jacket. "I'm sorry he never realized what he had in you, but you can't think like that. His loss."

"You're a good man, Luke."

He exited the truck and coerced the dog out. "You thinking I'm a good man has kept me going on more than a few nights."

A resigned sigh filtered through his phone. "Your wife didn't know how lucky she was."

Tingles raced up his spine. "Thank you."

"I miss you."

"Let me in, and show me how much." He turned the knob on the front door; it opened to display every cranny in the house decked out in Christmas ornamentation. The woman could make a home out of any house. Elegant, festive, and rich. Macy's compared to the artificial three-foot Douglas fir standing on the end table in his tiny living room. "Where are you?" He removed his work boots, and Derby slumped against the doormat. "Upstairs or down?"

"I'm in...where are you? I'm upstairs. In the laundry room."

He turned off the phone and walked quickly, but quietly, up eighteen oak stairs toward the rush of a washing machine.

"Luke? Are you there?"

He heard Kimberley's sweet voice a split second before he saw her. She entered the hallway, oblivious to his presence, with a basket of clothes tucked under her right arm, and her telephone cradled at her ear in her left hand.

In a cropped, hooded sweatshirt and low rise yoga pants, she looked as casual as she had at the gym. The two dimples above her round posterior seemed to wink at him, and her hair, wildly bouncing against her shoulders, lured him closer. Despite the cold weather, her feet were bare, and her toes, painted.

"All's well that ends well," she muttered, turning off the phone and tossing it into the basket of clothes.

"That's what I always say."

She spun to face him, lips slightly parted and eyes wide, turned back, and continued along her path into what he assumed to be her bedroom.

Silently, he followed her, choosing his moment. And finally, when she placed the basket of clothes onto the pink-clad queen-sized bed and reached for an article to fold, the moment arrived.

He shrugged out of his jacket and wrapped his arms around her, from back to front.

She flinched and spun toward him in surprise, a tiny pair of leggings dangling from her hand, but before she said a single word, he placed his mouth on hers.

Her lips parted, and she sank into the kiss.

He lowered her to the mattress, his hands sliding under her shirt, cupping her breasts in his hands, gently pushing them out of her bra. Full, firm, and fabulous. "It's been too long," he said pressing his hardening body between her thighs.

Her hands worked at his fly, popping the button, inching down the zipper. Unable to believe she was actually undressing him, he pulled his lips from her mouth and opened his eyes. Oh, yes. It was happening, all right.

"Hi," she breathed through a tender sigh.

"Hi." He peeled off her shirt, feathering his hands against her pretty skin, and whisked away her pants. "God, you look incredible." White lace undergarments; rosy nipples peeking up at him, her defined—but not too cut—abdomen beckoning to him.

Now exposed, he pressed his erection at her panties, rubbing impatiently against the silk, dropping kisses over her neck.

"Are you going to take them off, or work around them?" she whispered.

What? Oh, the panties. At the moment, he couldn't remember whether she was wearing them or not, and it didn't matter. Her warm, wet heat filtered through the length of him, panties or none. "You want them off?" He slid a hand under her rear and raked the panties from her body.

She propped her legs on his left shoulder, lifting her hips and enabling him to remove the lingerie completely, and lowered her legs around his waist.

He looked down at her opening, an unbelievably rare sight. He wanted to dive into it, to bury his lips in her soft, black hair, to rub his tongue against her g-spot and drink from her.

She pulled him closer. "Do you have anything?"

Besides a rock-hard cock and a yearning so far beyond desire he'd probably explode before entering her? His gaze darted to hers like magnets. "Anything?"

"Like a condom?"

"I'll brave the consequences."

"Wait." She fumbled in the nightstand drawer, and he kicked off his jeans and yanked the socks from his feet.

While she tore at a three-pack of condoms, opening it with her teeth, he pressed a finger into her. She melted over his flesh when he contacted the spot that months ago had turned her to pudding; he imagined his cock inside of her instead.

She whispered dreamily against his lips—something about luck—and writhed subtly beneath him, stroking a condom over him.

He closed his eyes, savoring the feeling of her hands on him. "I can't wait. I need you."

Without a word, she pressed the tip of his cock into her vagina and pressed her pelvis against him. "I can't believe how good it is." The rip in his T-shirt grew when she tore it from his body.

With one hand, he lifted her body under his, pulled back the covers with the other, and shifted her to the middle of the bed.

The laundry basket tumbled to the floor.

He shuddered in pleasure, deep inside the body he'd been unable to forget since the first time he'd laid eyes on her. A delicate hand trailed up his stomach and came to rest on his heart. Gazes locked, he placed his hand atop hers. No wedding ring. He embraced her tight to his torso. She was free. And for the moment, his.

He rolled her over and positioned her on top, her hot labia melting over his balls.

She kneaded her hips against his pelvis and pushed against his chest, rising an inch or two above him. A glistening of sweat tickled between their bodies, energized by the sudden filtering of air between them, refreshing, like morning dew. "Did you know this was going to happen?"

He shook his head. "Did you?"

"Yes," she whispered into another kiss.

A bra strap slipped from her shoulder.

He unclasped and removed her bra. Her nipples nestled in the sparse hair on his chest, and her thighs tightened astride him.

"I'm sorry," she breathed into his ear.

"About what?" He locked his lips around her mouth, feeling her cunt and tongue flex against him at the same time. His mind whirled as if a hurricane were about to roar through his brain. He held her in a taut, quivering embrace, pressing hard against her body, filling her to capacity, and spilling his load into her just when she shivered in a simultaneous peak.

He pumped his softening penis inside of her, and twitched up, ready to do it all again.

"That was a three-pack?"

"Yeah."

"We'll tear through the whole box before dinner, at this rate."

A breathy giggle escaped her.

"I'm gonna get you pregnant," he said between kisses.

"You say that as if you want to."

"*You* say *that* as if I've ever told you any different."

"How can you know? How do you know we'll be right together?"

"God, how could this be wrong?" He tugged on a wild curl and brushed it behind her ear.

She rolled off him. "We were pretty good, weren't we?" She lay on her back, one foot resting across his ankle, the rest of her body loose against the rumpled sheets.

"Yeah." He stroked her just under her breasts and groaned, her satiny skin invigorating him below the belt. Oh, to touch a woman freely again, to feel her respond. "And not only the sex."

Her gaze, misty and solemn, momentarily met his. "I'm sorry for the way things happened with us. Cheating, running around like that. How can I expect you to trust me after the way we—"

"Can you trust me?"

"I don't know."

"I guess we'll have to find out."

"Part of me is afraid to try."

When would the Discovery Channel report on the success rate of second marriages? "You can't be afraid forever. We deserve a chance."

She fingered the scar at his left eye. "What happened, here?"

"Saudi Arabia."

"I always wondered." She caressed the mark, concern in her expression. "I can't get over you again."

"So don't get over me." He pressed a hand to her abdomen. "And maybe someday I'll give you a reason not to."

She licked her lips and dragged a soft finger along his chin. "Someday."

"Maybe." He moved his fingers in slow circles against her tummy. "This might not be so bad, you know."

"How about one step at a time?"

"Great idea, beautiful girl. I'll take you to dinner tonight."

"A date?"

"Call it our first, the way it should've happened."

"Haven't been on one of those in a long time." Her smile brightened her already brilliant green eyes.

He sighed with the stroke of her hand, moving downward, along his jugular and across his chest. "We'll do things right this time. I want to spend some time with Allie. I'd like you to get to know my boy. And

Rachael, too."

She tickled his hips... "I'd like that." ...and stroked the condom off his hardening seven-and-five-eighths. "But that's not until next weekend."

"Never stop touching me." He groaned and rolled toward her. "We'll take it slow this time around, but promise me you'll never stop touching me."

"I like touching you. And I like it slow."

"I have something for you." He reached to the floor, into the pocket of his discarded flannel jacket and presented the velvet box to her.

Reluctantly, she took it. "Luke, I don't need things like this. You didn't have—"

"It's just a little something, reminded me of you, so... If you don't like it, you don't have to wear it."

She opened the box, and a genuine smile touched her lips. "I love it." She extracted the thin chain from its satin bed. "Help me with the clasp."

He fastened the delicate jewelry around her small wrist. "You're beautiful, you know that?"

She fingered the clover charm. "My new most flattering moment."

Had her skin always been this ivory, like a porcelain doll's? Her eyes as green as emeralds? "How did I get so lucky to find you?"

"You aren't lucky." She licked her lips and touched his scar again. "But I am."

PENNY DAWN

All right, so who among us doesn't have a few demons to exorcise?

Penny Dawn began her writing career at the tender age of seven, before she realized it's impossible to be All Good, All the Time...at least in the religious sense (grinning like a Cheshire.) Romantic stories with passionate twists have since become this Good Girl's forte...and she unleashes her demons on paper, over and over and over again.

Penny Dawn holds a B. A. in history and English from Northern Illinois University and is presently pursuing her M. A. in Creative Writing at Seton Hill University, whose alumnae include spicy novelists Jacki King, Shannon Hollis, Suzanne Forster, Dana Marton, and others. When she isn't writing, Penny enjoys tap, ballet, and jazz dance, photography, physical fitness, and renovating her 1906 Victorian Lady with her husband and two daughters.

Drop by her website www.pennydawn.com to discuss all things decadent.

AMBER QUILL PRESS, LLC
THE GOLD STANDARD IN PUBLISHING

QUALITY BOOKS
IN BOTH PRINT AND ELECTRONIC FORMATS

ACTION/ADVENTURE	SUSPENSE/THRILLER
SCIENCE FICTION	PARANORMAL
MAINSTREAM	MYSTERY
FANTASY	EROTICA
ROMANCE	HORROR
HISTORICAL	WESTERN
YOUNG ADULT	NON-FICTION

AMBER QUILL PRESS, LLC
http://www.amberquill.com

Made in the USA